falling for

forester

cole & crys

book 3

RENEE VINCENT

FALLING FOR FORESTER: (COLE & CRYS)
Copyright © 2016, Renee Vincent
Digital ISBN: 978-1-94448-401-9
Trade Paperback ISBN: 978-1-94448-402-6

Cover Art Design by Renee Vincent
Stock Art by BigStock.com
Editor, Linda Ingmanson

Digital Release: May, 2016
Trade Paperback Release: May, 2016

For the members of my Street Team,

I cannot thank you enough for all the support you give, and the time you set aside to read, review, and recommend my work. I'm very lucky to have the best Street Team in the world!

FALLING FOR FORESTER
Mavericks of Meeteetse, Book 3 (Cole & Crys)

Best friend and fellow cowboy cattle rancher Cole Forester likes things the way they are—quiet, no-frills, and uncomplicated. He's a glorified bachelor with only a dog as his companion, totally content to live a solitary life next to the McKinley ranch. That is until a cute little barrel racer shows up looking for a job as a ranch hand.

Tomboy Crys Willingham hangs up her rodeo hat and heads to where her friend Ava Wallace lives, hoping to score a job that doesn't involve the risk of broken bones every time she mounts up. But once she lays eyes on Cole, it seems it's her vulnerable heart that's in danger of breaking.

Chapter One

It took everything Brody Galven had not to think about when his Liv would get on a plane and head back to Nashville. While he held her in his arms, he knew his time with her was limited and each moment twice as precious. He had no idea how he'd be able to say good-bye to her again when that day came.

For him, the past few weeks had been perfect, like the good old days, but better because they were no longer just childhood friends. They were best friends, deeply in love with each other.

Every day since she'd returned home to Meeteetse and surprised him with a phone call to say she was waiting on her mama's front porch, he picked her up after working on the McKinley ranch and took her wherever she wanted to go. Some days they went fishing in the Greybull River, or grabbed a bite to eat at the Wagon Wheel, where she used to waitress. But tonight, they lay lazily on a blanket in the bed of his truck, gazing up at the stars twinkling overhead.

He pulled her close, drawing in the scent of her hair: strawberry shampoo mixed with the sweet vanilla perfume he loved so much. "I missed this smell."

Olivia looked up from the cradle of his shoulder and met his gaze. "I missed this look in your eyes," she said, reaching up to touch his face. "This look that lets me know how much I've been on your mind."

He grasped her hand and kissed the inside of her wrist. "Not a moment goes by without the thought of you, Liv."

She closed her eyes and snuggled back into his embrace. "Do you ever think about the future?" She paused, then added, "Our future?"

"All the time. And it scares me."

Brody felt her body tense and wished he would've kept his feelings to himself. He didn't mean to sound cynical, as Liv had always been the one thing in his life he could count on. But now that she was chasing a dream, he didn't know if he could keep up with her. Or worse, perhaps she'd have no need for him once her success took her to even greater heights. Like his brother, Rod, had said once before, Olivia was now a bird with wings.

"Honestly, I'm scared too, Brody."

He rolled and faced her, cupping the back of her head in his palm. With his other hand, he caressed her beautiful face, finding it hard to believe that Liv was concerned about the unknown. She was a go-getter, a woman who never backed down from a challenge, even when the going got tough.

"When it comes to your singing career, you have nothing to be afraid of. You're going to make it big. I know this."

"And I want you to know this," Liv said, looking deep into his eyes. "No matter where I go, I take you with me. And no matter how far away I travel to sing for other people, I sing for you. You are all that matters to me. Without you, this dream means nothing."

He kissed her lips, soothing her heavy heart as much as he did his. "I'll always be here for you, Liv. I'm not going anywhere." A smile curved his lips, and he couldn't stop it. "Even though your mother wishes otherwise."

Liv smiled with him. "She doesn't feel that way."

"Oh yes, she does. And I don't blame her. June wants the best for her little girl. I only hope one day she realizes I'm nothing like her father...or yours."

"With time, she will."

"Lucky for me, I've got nothing but time. I'd spend forever proving your mother wrong if that's what it took."

Liv wrapped her arms around his neck and pressed her lips to his. "I'd rather you prove it to me. Starting right now."

Brody didn't have to be told twice. He slid his arms around her body and pulled her in tight. Nothing, he vowed, would come between them. Not June, not

Nashville, not anything.

Chapter Two

Nothing says damsel in distress like white smoke billowing from the hood of a full-sized pickup truck on the side of the road. And nothing wills a man to pull over like a nice curvy butt in jeans.

Cole Forester shot a quick glance in his rearview mirror before he decided to stop and help, taking in the length of the woman's blonde hair falling down her back. Much to his surprise, her beautiful golden locks stopped short of her low-rise denim belt loops. He tamped down a smile, pulled over, and threw the shifter into Park.

Looks like my crappy day is finally perking up.

Sammy, his Australian Blue Heeler, barked twice and sat up on the front seat beside him. Cole noticed he no longer struggled with rising to his feet, despite the long, gruesome scar running across his hind leg from a protective mama grizzly a few months ago. Doc Peterson had said it might take as long as six months for Sammy to heal. Cole was thrilled it had taken less.

He scratched Sammy behind the ears and commanded

him to stay. The dog whined once in protest but did as he was told.

Cole stepped out of the cab as he adjusted his cowboy hat. Steam still spewed from the radiator of her truck, which he noticed was a three-quarter-ton GMC with alloy wheels and a killer paint job, but the cute blonde was suddenly nowhere to be found.

He shut his truck door and pointed another warning to Sammy before walking toward her vehicle. He examined the scene. New truck. Texas plates. Matching horse trailer. And a disappearing lady in distress.

He'd heard the folks in Texas didn't mess around. With his luck, she probably ran inside her living quarters for a gun. When he brought to mind her small stature, he couldn't imagine one ounce of aggression in that sweet little body, much less a woman equipped to wield a firearm.

He walked around the passenger side of her truck and looked down the length of the rig behind it. By the time he peeked through the tinted cab windows, he heard the unmistakable sound of a pump-action shotgun behind him.

He froze and slowly raised his hands to shoulder level. "Easy, ma'am."

"I'll ease up after you get back in your truck and roll on, mister."

Cole smiled, entertained by the woman's bravery. At

six foot five, two hundred forty pounds, he was nothing to sneeze at. And based on the good look he got of her as he drove by, he figured she couldn't have been much taller than five foot seven.

"I don't blame you for being cautious in this day and age, little lady, but I'm harmless."

"Yeah, that's what they all say."

"They?"

"Rapists and murderers."

Cole scoffed. "Might I give you some advice? You shouldn't hang around people like that."

"You think you're funny?"

He did, but was mighty glad she couldn't see the grin on his face. She'd have pumped his butt full of lead.

"Call it a defense mechanism for having a gun pointed at my back. I'm only trying to be a gentleman."

"Unfortunately, I don't know you well enough to tell if you're lying. And the longer you stand here, the more suspicious I become of your Good Samaritan act. Consider this a fair warning. I know how to use this thing, I'm far from gullible, and I have trust issues."

You don't say.

"Look, I couldn't care less whether you believe me or not. But you're not going anywhere with that radiator overheating. You need fluid in that engine, and the closest place is about ten miles up the road. It's called the Wagon Wheel. Nice little place that serves cold drinks and hot bar food. I'm driving that way myself and wouldn't mind giving you a lift."

"It's kind of you, but I'll pass."

"You'll never make it without some sort of fluid to cool the engine, especially with that trailer. And it's a long way on foot."

"I've got a horse."

"At least tell me you have a phone—"

"Got that too. Should I call the police right now?"

Cole slowly turned around and looked at his stubborn adversary. She stood with her feet spread and gripped a gorgeous Remington Model 870 Wingmaster pump-action shotgun at her shoulder like a pro, unlike a novice who'd be hip-shooting.

Nice.

"Something else funny?"

He must have smiled, but he quickly erased it. "Not at all. I was just admiring your weapon of choice. Got one just like it."

"Then you know it's pretty lethal at close range. Not to mention it has a solid steel receiver and twin action bars for flawless cycling. It's an American icon that will take you down in the blink of an eye."

Cole didn't hide his amusement this time. She'd grabbed his attention with her sweet little bod but stole his heart with her proficient knowledge of firearms.

He could almost marry her.

A picture of them standing together at an altar beneath a rustic arbor of elk antlers popped into his head. She wore a simple white sundress, cowboy boots, and a scowl, much like the look she was giving him now.

"I do," he stated, "know all that and more about the Remington."

"Good. Now, please don't make me prove it."

"Yes, ma'am." He watched her step to the side, giving him room to move between her and her truck. Her sights remained on him.

Keeping his hands raised, he held her gaze as he slipped past. While glad to leave in one piece, part of him was disappointed he hadn't snagged her name. It wasn't often a woman like that waltzed into his world. Most were typical powder-and-paint chicks whose expertise lay in accessorizing and lip gloss application. This one was a genuine cowgirl with piss and vinegar running through her veins. She had a free, untamable spirit and a big Texas ego, for neither of which she'd ever apologize. Like the crisp mountain breeze of Wyoming, she was truly a breath of fresh air.

Staring down the barrel, he backed up all the way to his truck and climbed inside. Sammy remained quiet and submissive, greeting him only with a happy tail wag as he tugged the shifter into Drive. From his view in the side mirror, he could see she kept aim. He pinched the brim of his hat and nodded a polite cowboy farewell at her reflection before pulling away.

Driving off proved harder than he expected. She'd made a considerable impression on him, and he hated that he'd never see her again. Against his better judgment, he glanced at his rear mirrors from time to time. He fought the urge to tromp down on the brakes and spin a U-ee.

Was he crazy?

Was he trying to get himself killed?

She's a girl, made of gunpowder and lead who'd love a good excuse to prove it.

Sammy nuzzled next to him as if he sensed his discontentment. Cole absently stroked his fur, mulling over his options. Essentially, he had none. Whether she fascinated him or not, he couldn't go back there without the risk of getting shot.

Sammy barked, jerking Cole's focus away from the long stretch of blacktop behind him. He pulled his dog closer and patted him soundly. "You're right. She ain't worth it. Besides, women only complicate things, don't they?"

Sammy acknowledged him with another yap and offered his paw. Cole laughed and shook it, pretending to accept the dog's proposition.

"Deal. Only a bachelor's life for us."

Chapter Three

Crys Willingham leaned against the front bumper of her truck, staring at the silver tailgate of some guy's GMC as he drove off toward the Absaroka Mountain Range. He wasn't just any guy. He was a distinctly handsome, lumberjack sort of fellow with dark hair and chocolate-brown eyes. He had a clear, deep voice that resembled the sultry timbre of her favorite country singer, Josh Turner, and an adorable smile.

She'd seen her fair share of good-looking cowboys in Texas. Being born into a family of championship bull riders, and the youngest sibling of three brothers, hot, cocky cowboys were a dime a dozen. But this one was without a doubt the most beautiful man she'd ever seen.

She grinned, thinking about his casual demeanor, even when she'd pumped a round into the chamber. Most men would've shit themselves. This cowboy didn't seem fazed in the least. Either he'd been held at gunpoint way too many times in his life, or he didn't think she'd pull the trigger.

No matter what the reason, his offhand confidence stuck in her mind longer than his exceptional good looks—a first for her.

Crys looked over her shoulder at the engine. The smoke had dispersed, but she knew better than to drive away. Like the cute cowboy had said, she ran the risk of blowing the engine if she drove much farther without fluid.

If her three brothers had taught her anything, it was the importance of maintaining a well-oiled machine with regular tune-ups. Since she'd topped off all the fluids before she left Houston, she dreaded that something was wrong. Her brand-new truck should've had no trouble hauling her three-horse trailer, especially since there was only one horse in it.

She pulled out her cell and headed back to the trailer to put her shotgun away. As she stepped inside, she scrolled through until she found her friend's number. She sat down at the kitchen booth and laid the shotgun across the table. The trailer rocked just enough to let her know her horse was getting impatient. Luckily, it was cool autumn day, and she didn't have to worry about Jericho withstanding the heat from the afternoon sun.

"McKinley Ranch and Riding Stables, this is Rhonda, may I help you?"

Crys hesitated. She didn't expect anyone besides her friend to answer. "Uh, yes. May I speak to Ava Wallace?"

"May I ask who's calling?"

"Sure. This is Crys Willingham. We used to ride the rodeo circuit together—"

"Yes, yes, Crystal Willingham! Ava said you'd be calling once you reached town. You're the champion barrel racer, right?"

Crys smiled, humbled that the woman knew her name. "At one time I was, yeah. But it's been a few years since I've been in the limelight."

"Honey, when you reach my age, the only limelight you'll get is in a dentist chair." After they shared a laugh, Rhonda continued to ask questions. "I hear you're moving up this way from Texas."

"That *is* the plan."

"It must be so exciting for you," Rhonda exclaimed. "Traveling all over the country. Going wherever the wind takes you."

Crys kicked back in her seat, surprised by how much Ava had shared with Rhonda about her sudden desire to hang up the rodeo life. It was true she loved roaming from place to place, but life on the road eventually took its toll. She was tired of sleeping on a cheap camper mattress, sick of food from a microwave, and finished with men trying to run her life—her father and brothers included.

No one thought she'd actually drop everything and leave Houston. She'd always been the one to stick it out because of loyalty, even if it wasn't in her best interest. For as long as she could remember, she did what made her father proud, what made her manager happy and her brothers content. It was time she lived her own life.

"As exciting as living on the road can be, I'm looking forward to hanging up my hat somewhere. Settling down, that kind of thing."

"In Meeteetse, maybe?" Rhonda intimated.

Crys had no idea where. All she knew was she wanted to live in a small town where the sky was big and life was slow—the complete opposite of Houston.

To find it, she'd been driving up Interstate 25 from New Mexico to Wyoming. She thought she found a place in Fort Collins. Rich in western lore, it had drawn her in with all its charm and mountainous landscape, but the area was too hip and modern for her taste.

Cheyenne held the appeal as home of the largest outdoor rodeo in the nation, but lost Crys's favor once she realized the "Magic City of the Plains" was too much like home.

For a time, Big Horn, Wyoming had seemed like the perfect place to hang her hat, until she talked to Ava last week. Once her friend had mentioned Meeteetse, the town "Where Chiefs Meet," she felt she needed to, at least, check it out. Packing up, she hit Highway 14 into Cody and headed south, never thinking she'd break down.

"Maybe Meeteetse. Maybe Big Horn. I haven't decided yet."

"I trust Wyoming is treating you good so far?"

"Well, that's the problem. I'm kind of stuck in Wyoming whether I like it or not. It seems my truck's having issues with the thin air up here."

"Oh, dear. Where are you?"

Without having her GPS up and running, Crys based her whereabouts on the sexy stranger's knowledge. "I think I'm just north of Meeteetse on Highway 120, roughly ten miles from the Wagon Wheel? Ever heard of it? I've not been there, but some cutie patootie cowboy mentioned it by name. He told me it was the closest place to civilization."

"And he didn't stay to help you?" Rhonda's tone flipped from bubbly to critical in a split second. "He stopped to tell you where you were but didn't offer his assistance? Cute or not, he doesn't sound like much of a cowboy to me."

An image of the man popped in Crys's head: his dusty boots, his tight, worn-out jeans, and his black felt hat that could've used both a good cleaning and a heavy steaming. She'd seen many wannabes in her day, but this guy was not one of them. He was a genuine cowboy through and through.

"Oh, he tried his best to lend a hand," Crys said, sticking up for the fellow, "but I wasn't all that comfortable. Being a woman alone in the middle of nowhere, I told him I didn't need his help."

"The man left you stranded anyway? I'd like to stick my boot in his ass for that," Rhonda mumbled.

Without meeting Rhonda, Crys concluded she could take a likin' to her. Any woman who dared to kick some guy's butt was her kind of people. "Don't be so hard on the guy. If not for my twelve-gauge, I'm sure he would've stuck around longer."

Crys heard Rhonda cackle on the other end. "Ava wasn't lying. You *are* one tough cookie. Hold on, I'll go fetch her. I think she's in the barn."

"Thanks."

While Crys waited, she stood and looked out the window of her trailer. Not a single car had passed since the gentleman cowboy had driven off. She was definitely in a remote area of Wyoming—just the kind of place she was looking for. In Houston, one would be lucky to find remote. It was the most populated city in Texas, and even though her family resided on a secluded thirteen-acre farm about an hour from downtown, the outskirts of the town were still a well-traveled region.

"Crys? Crys, you there?"

"Hey, Ava! Sorry to bother you. I know you're busy."

"No, you're not a bother at all. What's going on? Rhonda said you're broke down? Whereabouts are you?"

Crys could hear the panic in Ava's voice. "It's just a little radiator trouble. Nothing huge, I think."

She hoped.

New diesel trucks were known for their dependable, long-lasting engines, but when something went wrong, it was often costly. "Any chance you could meet me out here with some coolant?"

"Of course, I can. Do we need to tow your truck? It's not a problem if you think it's best."

"Actually, I think I need someone to tow my trailer. With this radiator on the fritz, I'd like to spare the engine. Lighten its load if we can."

"You got it. Which trailer did you bring? The gooseneck or the bumper pull?"

"Goose."

"All right, give me a few minutes to pack up."

"While you're at it, why don't you pack up that sexy boy-toy cattle rancher you've been hoarding for yourself and bring him with you. I haven't seen him in ages."

Ava chuckled. "You mean Jonas?"

"Yes, I mean Jonas. What's Mr. Sweet Tush doing these days besides knocking boots with you?"

"Ah, Crystal, you haven't changed a bit, have you?"

"Neither have you. You're still trying to change the subject whenever I bring up the topic of sex."

Crys heard Ava shuffling around on the other end of the line. She figured Ava was probably rooting around for jugs of antifreeze to bring to Crys's rescue.

That was Ava. All work and no play.

She and Crys were total opposites, which was likely the reason they got along so well. The extreme poles of their personalities balanced each other.

"You listening to me, Ava?" Crys prodded. "There's no sense in hiding the fact you're having sex with that stud, McKinley. Heck, most of the entire female race is still ticked at you for taking him off the market."

A nervous laugh stuttered from Ava. "Then I guess they won't be too happy now that he's my fiancé."

"Nuh-uh!" Crys could hardly believe it. With the considerable age gap between Ava and Jonas, it had always been hard to take their relationship seriously. Though she always wanted the best for Ava, she often warned her friend not to get too hung up on him. Never in a million years would she have thought Meeteetse's most eligible bachelor would settle down—nor tie the knot with a woman ten years older than him. "You mean to tell me he finally popped the question after all these years? What's it been, six?"

"Seven," Ava corrected. "But who's counting?"

"I bet you were."

"Actually, no. I can't say that I was."

Crys heard the drawn-out pause at the end of Ava's statement. Perhaps Ava had regretted saying yes to Jonas's proposal. As far as Crys was concerned, there was still time to back out. She didn't want to see Ava jumping into an arrangement based on convenience or social standards. "But?"

"But...I'm very happy he took that leap. I can't imagine spending the rest of my life with anyone but Jonas."

Crys plopped her butt back down on the cushioned seat of the kitchen dinette. All this sappy love talk suffocated her. She enjoyed knowing her friend had roped herself a cowboy as sexy and successful as Jonas McKinley. But relationships, and all the unnecessary effort to make them work, were not for her.

"You can keep your marriage, and your white picket fence. Sooner or later, you'll get bored—or worse, cowboy

McKinley'll get bored and want a newer model." As soon as it came out of her mouth, Crys realized she'd insulted Ava. "No offense."

"None taken…I think." A long awkward silence spanned the call until Ava broke in with a sharp intake of breath. "Well, just so you know, that isn't going to happen between me and Jonas. His love for me is real. And one day, you'll find that too. I know you will."

Crys didn't put much stock in finding a Prince Charming anytime soon. "I'll stick with my horse, Jericho. He's the only male who doesn't tell me how to live my life or get jealous when I decide to mount some other steed. He doesn't even complain about eating the same old grain day after day. Now, that's love."

"On some level, sure. But don't you ever miss the camaraderie? The long talks over dinner? The comfort of knowing someone is there for you no matter what?"

"That's what girl friends are for."

Ava laughed in her usual sweet way. "So, does that mean you're swearing off men altogether?"

"Hell, no. I still want a man to warm my bed every now and again. Just not the same one every time. Now quit trying to domesticate me and get your butt here. Jericho's been in the back of the trailer long enough."

The one thing that would get Ava moving was a horse

in need, and Crys used it to her advantage without regret.

"Right. Right. Jericho. I'm on my way."

"Don't forget the coolant," Crys reminded.

"It's already in my truck. I need to find Jonas and let him know where I'm going. Once I'm on the road, I'll call you back and we can figure out where you are exactly. If you're about ten miles north of the Wagon Wheel like Rhonda mentioned, I have a pretty good idea."

Crys admired how proficient Ava was with every task she undertook. She gave concise explanations, and she was always one step ahead of the game. She had a way of making you feel like everything would be okay, no matter what the dilemma. Ava Wallace would get you through.

For Crys, that meant everything at this point in her life. She needed a female role model who was both supportive and encouraging. A confidante who'd not forego the importance of independence. A friend who valued loyalty till the end.

Raised by her father and her three bull-riding brothers—all of whom she knew meant well—Crys had never had a nurturing, maternal influence growing up. Within a male-dominated household, all she came to know was how to make it in a man's world, how to drop said man to his knees with one throat punch, and how to suppress her emotions. Anything construed as weak had to go.

For a time, those were valuable life lessons. She had learned to be resilient, self-reliant, and formidable in the face of opposition. But after years of bending to her family's will, she was ready to go her own way.

With two hundred grand in her pocket and everything she owned in her truck and trailer, Crys had her sights set on a new life. A life where she had both hands on the wheel.

Excited, and a little uneasy about being on her own—terrified, actually—she gathered her bravado and sat up straighter in her seat. "Ava?" she prompted, then cleared her throat. "Thank you...for dropping everything and coming to get me."

For a moment, Crys thought the call had dropped, as there was dead silence on the line. Before she could ask if Ava was still there, Ava spoke with emotion in her voice.

"Crystal. You've always been there for me. It's the least I can do."

Chapter Four

Cole slid the last bag of minerals from the bed of his truck to the tailgate and heaved it upon his shoulder. With autumn in full swing, he and fellow rancher, Jonas McKinley, were busy stocking up on feed and supplements for the livestock on the McKinley ranch.

Though each owned their own separate acreage, Cole and Jonas shared a fifty-fifty split of the responsibilities and profits from the cattle business. They were widely known for their quality Angus steers, raised for both the meat and rodeo industries.

As it stood, they supplied young steers for all the bovine events at many of the nation's rodeos, large and small, and preparation was year-round. To comply with the Professional Rodeo Cowboys Association regulations, each steer used had to be healthy, strong, and between two hundred twenty and two hundred eighty pounds. Maintaining this weight during the harsh winter weather, when the quality of forage drops, often required an increase in supplements, protein, and a round of wormer.

Cole and Jonas prided themselves on the work they did with these animals. And while it sometimes wore him down, Cole enjoyed the outdoor labor. He wouldn't last one day sitting at a desk in a stuffy, tight-closed cubicle.

As he carried the fifty-pound bag into Jonas's barn, he felt a twinge in his lower back. He flipped the bag on the top of the stack and reached for the strain in his lumbar, stretching it out.

"Taking up yoga in your spare time now?"

Cole turned around just in time to see Jonas carrying a Styrofoam box of meds that Cole had bought at Tractor Farm Supply in Cody. "Yeah. That's what I'm doing. Yoga."

Jonas put the meds in the barn refrigerator. "You look more like a Pilates guy to me."

Cole frowned. "I don't even know what that is."

"Me neither. But Ava's been talking about taking a class on it. Thinks I should do it with her."

There was no thinking about it. By the look on Jonas's face, Cole could tell that Ava had already signed them both up, whether he liked it or not. "So when do you start, Mary?"

Jonas rolled his eyes. "Next Tuesday night. And I'm not thrilled about it."

"Then don't go."

Jonas huffed and shot him *the look*. "That's not an option."

Cole crossed his arms, surprised by his friend's gutlessness. "Sure it is."

"You think that because you've never been in a steady relationship. But trust me, when you care about a woman, the last thing you want to do is disappoint her. Sometimes her happiness is all that matters."

"Even at the expense of yours? No thanks."

After hearing Jonas's explanation for why a man should suck it up and take orders from the woman in the relationship, it only affirmed his mind-set. A bachelor's life was far better than being chained to a dictator with boobs. Not that he thought Ava was a tyrant—she was a lovely woman, with a very nice rack. But that didn't mean kick-ass curves trumped his independence.

He treasured his freedom too much to give it up. He was a creature of habit, and a man of prerogative. If he wanted Chinese for breakfast, then by God, he'd eat Chinese. If he drank so much that he passed out on the floor, so be it. If he dated two women at the same time, more power to him.

He was his own man, with his own life, and no woman was going to tell him how he should live it.

"One day you'll see it my way," Jonas said, patting him on the back as they walked toward Cole's truck.

"It'll be a cold day in hell, McKinley." Cole closed the tailgate and scanned the yard for his dog. It wasn't like Sammy to run off farther than eyeshot. "Have you seen Sam?"

Jonas looked around. "He was here when I walked up. Oh, look, there he is. He's waiting at the gate for Ava to pull in."

Cole gazed down the gravel drive, taking note of the strange three-horse trailer Ava had hitched to her truck. Sammy barked in delight and ran alongside the vehicle, anxious to greet her.

"Did you get a new horse trailer?"

"No, that's Ava's friend's trailer. Crys Willingham. Evidently, she broke down on the side of the road making the trip up from Houston. Radiator problems, I think Ava said. I don't know, I was too busy greasing the fittings on the tractor to really listen. That's her pulling in behind Ava."

Cole recognized the Sundowner trailer and the shiny black GMC from earlier this afternoon. His heart kicked up a notch when he saw the gorgeous blonde in the driver's seat of that stylish four-by-four, looking as pretty as a peach.

I'll be damned.

She parked below the big horse barn next to Ava's truck, and within seconds, she hopped out of the cab to meet Ava at the back of her trailer. Sammy made quick work of the woman's scent and deemed her harmless. He greeted her with a round of exuberate yips as she bent to pet him.

Cole noticed how her long hair fell off her shoulders, tempting him to take hold of it by the fistful. As he stood there fixating on her beauty, he practically saw himself tugging on those silky strands right before he kissed her senseless.

Unnerved by his wild, impulsive thoughts, he stuffed his hands in the pockets of his Carhartt jacket.

What was he doing?

She was Ava's friend, completely untouchable as far as he was concerned.

Cole hardly mingled and rarely dated. But if he took a woman to his bed, his friends couldn't know her beforehand in any fashion—whatsoever. If she was familiar to them by either friendship or blood, she was inarguably off limits.

No exceptions.

He didn't have many restrictions in his life, but the few he had were for his own good. Adhering to them helped him avoid trouble and shun unnecessary drama.

No matter how hard he tried to convince himself that she wasn't worth the hassle, he couldn't help but imagine the possibilities. They had lots in common—their love for quarter horses, jacked-up trucks, and legendary guns. It seemed like a match made in heaven, until he remembered staring down the barrel of that renowned Remington. A woman who wielded a firearm like a sharpshooter wasn't looking down her steel sights so much for a tryst but for a target.

Cole swallowed hard and drew in a slow breath. He tried not to undress her with his eyes, but that was all he could think about.

"...it might be as soon as this week, but I'll let you know."

Cole blinked and tore his attention away from Ava's friend. "What?" He hadn't realized he'd zoned out, until he saw the wide-eyed look on Jonas's face. "You'll let me know what?"

Jonas drew back. "When the fall calves drop. From the herd of mamas we bred to the new bull we bought last winter. Were you even listening to me?"

"Right. Right. Right. New bull. New calves." Cole's mind sped forward, recalling their trial run with a low-birth-weight, high-wean-weight bull. "I got it. They're ready to drop. Possibly this week."

Jonas narrowed his gaze as if he were trying to figure out the cause for Cole's momentary lapse of focus. "Everything all right?" He glanced toward Ava's friend, who was in the process of backing her horse out of the trailer. "Someone got your mind on the fritz? I mean, if you're interested in meeting her, I can surely introduce—"

"No, no, no. I gotta run. I was just waiting for her to safely back that horse off the trailer before I pulled out." Cole whistled for Sammy and opened his truck door.

"You sure? She's awful cute. A little spitfire, barrel racer I hear. Right up your alley."

"I'll pass. I've got that no-friends-and-family rule," Cole reminded as he climbed in the cab behind Sammy and turned the key.

Jonas peered at him through the open truck window. "Rules are made to be broken, you know."

Cole shook his head and adjusted his cowboy hat to sit low on his brow. "Not mine. I'm a firm believer in them. For good reason."

He looked over his shoulder to make sure Ava and Crys were clear out of sight before throwing the gear in Drive. He figured it was best to leave without the blonde recognizing him from their encounter this afternoon.

"Tell Ava I said hey."

"Sure thing, Forester. Although you know she's going to wonder why you jetted out so fast."

Cole threw Jonas his best whatever smirk and drove on without missing a beat.

Chapter Five

Crys led Jericho into the empty stall Ava had offered to let her use during her stay, and as she stepped out into the aisle of the barn, she caught sight of a vehicle leaving the premises. While it was the same silver GMC she'd noticed when she first arrived at the McKinley ranch, she still couldn't make out its owner—only the dog she'd met moments ago, now hanging out the passenger window. She wondered if that was the same cowboy hottie who'd pulled over this afternoon to offer assistance.

Wouldn't that be awkward?

She didn't recall the cowboy having a dog, though. Then again, she hadn't paid much attention to anything but his gorgeous face and his muscular build as she'd zeroed in on him through steel sights.

While her mind turned over the possibilities, Ava placed a half bale of hay in the rack for Jericho to munch on and patted his hindquarters on the way out. After closing the heavy pine door behind him, she dusted off her hands and smiled.

"So," Ava huffed, matching Crys's joy with a sparkle in her eyes. "If you need more stall bedding, there are shavings under the overhang at this end of the barn. Scoop shovels and wheelbarrows are there too." Ava turned and pointed toward the opposite end of the horse barn. "The manure pit's outside, next to the woodshed. It's kind of a far walk, but it's easier to access with the skid steer bucket when we need to empty it."

Crys smiled, warmed by the fact that Ava felt the need to apologize for any inconveniences she'd endure on the ranch. If anyone was going to be inconvenienced, it would be Jonas and Ava for letting her stay a few weeks on their farm. "I appreciate you opening your home to me."

Ava reached out and touched her shoulder. "It's no trouble. In fact, I'm thrilled you accepted my offer to check out Meeteetse. I really think you'll like it here." Ava paused with a look of expectation on her face. "Do you know how long you plan to stay?"

Crys scratched the back of her neck, uncertain of her own plans. "A coupla weeks. Maybe a month…if it's not too much to ask?"

"Stay as long as you like, Crys. I mean that." Ava bit her lip and glanced outside the barn at Crys's horse trailer. "Are you sure you won't reconsider sleeping in the house?

You are more than welcome to—"

"Absolutely not. I didn't come here to be a burden."

"You won't be."

Crys knew she had to be firm yet gentle with Ava. Though she was a strong believer in a woman's independence, Ava was also a tenderhearted soul. Crys blamed that on motherhood. "I can't thank you enough for everything you've done, but I'll be fine in my trailer. I've got every amenity I could ever need, you know that. How many weeks on end did we spend living in our trailers, traveling from show to show? As long as we had heat and running water, we were good to go."

"I know, but…"

"No buts about it. I'm here to find out if Meeteetse is a place I could call home, and not to invade yours in the process. Now, let's get this Willingham Waldorf unhooked from your truck and leveled, huh?"

Ava conceded, and together they worked to get Crys all set up. Crys climbed into the back of Ava's truck and unhooked the latches and chains from the ball hitch. Ava stood at the driver's side of the trailer and worked the hydraulic jack to raise the nose of the goose while Crys pulled her truck out from under it. Without prompting, the two of them took care of leveling the trailer, hooking it up to water and electric, and mucking the back end, just like in the good old days. They joked and shared horse stories, some of which involved moments of near-death experiences with crazy ones, and reminisced about a few wild cowboys from their rodeo days. It was as if time had never passed between them.

Catching up with Ava meant so much to Crys. She'd never really had a close relationship with anyone, especially since she'd grown up with three protective older brothers and a domineering father. It was an all-work-and-no-play kind of upbringing, and she'd hated every minute of it. Though she loved her family deeply and understood that they only wanted the best for her career, she was glad to be rid of both her kin and the barrel racing profession that had practically sucked the life out of her. She'd made her stand by leaving town and starting her life anew.

Was she afraid she'd fail at this thing called life? Darn tootin'. But at least she could say she did so without regret. Starting today, she'd only look ahead and swear to live life to its fullest.

****

Crys finished washing her hands at the bathroom sink inside the McKinley abode and came out admiring its warm, rustic atmosphere. A quaint guestroom and office divided the hall, while a luxurious bedroom, trimmed in deep violets and silver, opened off the living room. The rest of the home was a modest yet open floor plan, with gorgeous pinewood planks lining the walls and a richer hickory hardwood making up the floors. The only thing spacious, Crys noticed, was the wraparound porch encircling the charming ranch-style log home.

Upon entering the dining area, Crys sat at an open seat at the table. Jonas sat at the head, his hands crossed as he waited for Ava to join them from the kitchen. She regarded his quiet demeanor and his polite attire, realizing it was the first time she'd ever seen him without his cowboy hat. Though his hair stood tousled on top and depressed around the sides from a hat's daily use, he still looked as handsome as ever.

"I hope you like meatloaf," Ava said as she set a basket of rolls between them and took a seat across from Crys.

A whole spread of piping-hot food lay before her. Boiled red potatoes, a bowl of buttery corn, and a platter of homegrown Angus beef filled her nostrils with heavenly goodness.

"Are you kidding?" Crys said, her mouth nearly watering. "I can't remember the last time I had meatloaf. It was probably more than twenty years ago, when my mom was still in the picture."

A hush fell over the table, and Crys inwardly cringed that she'd brought up her late mother in such an offhand comment. "Sorry. Sometimes I just blurt things out."

"It's okay," Ava said, still squirming to get out from under the awkwardness. "You can say anything here. We won't judge."

Crys laughed at Ava's attempt to smooth it over. "At any rate, I'm very grateful for all the trouble you went through to cook for me while I took care of my horse."

"Speaking of, do you have enough hay? I noticed you had about seven bales with you, so if you're staying longer than a couple of weeks, you're more than welcome to have some of ours."

Crys noticed the covert glance Ava shared with Jonas. He gave no indication that he objected, but she wanted to assure him she'd not be a freeloader during her visit. "I'll accept as long as you let me buy them from you."

Ava crossed her arms and sat back in her chair. She'd not win this battle with Crys. "If you must, but please know that Jonas and I do not expect you to pay for every little thing. You're our guest."

"Ava's right," Jonas finally spoke. "You're our guest, and we want you to feel at home."

Crys felt the subtle tension leave the room, and it was all because Jonas had harmonized with Ava's gracious hospitality. Little did he know, she needed that. She'd been so used to winning the approval of men in her life that she'd looked for it, even now. Somehow, she was determined to change that way of thinking.

"Now let's say grace before this food gets cold." Jonas winked.

Crys folded her hands in prayer and listened to the words Jonas spoke in gratefulness. He not only thanked the good Lord for the delicious meal they were about to eat, but the many blessings of his life, which included his beloved Ava. Crys wasn't accustomed to formal prayer but enjoyed the pure comfort it gave her, especially when everything else was so up in the air.

Throughout dinner, small talk ensued, and easy laughter soon followed. They talked of Ava's mishaps on the ranch, including the time she accidently fell in the water trough in an attempt to seduce her cowboy, and then Jonas's proposal thereafter. When the subject eventually fell to Crys and her family, she spoke fondly of her brothers' successes in the PBR, and her father's recent second marriage. So as not to air out her laundry again, she refrained from mentioning the gold-digging wife and her repulsive age of twenty-six next to her father's sixty-seven.

At the close of the meal, Ava opened a bottle of wine and Jonas popped a beer. They moved from the table to the couch, chatting comfortably in front of a log fire that Jonas had built in the rock fireplace. Their conversation then switched to the cattle and horseback riding business, the different facets of the McKinley ranch, and those who worked it to make it a success.

By Ava's second glass of wine, she acquired a talent for giggling and brainstorming. Crys, on the other hand, nursed her first glass, all the while wishing she'd been offered a cold beer.

Ava continued to bump her gums about the hired hands and their extreme loyalty for working alongside her and Jonas for so many years. Jonas sat in the leather chair, sipping his beer. He didn't say much, but Crys could tell by the way he gazed upon his fiancée that he loved and admired her. For Crys, that was more interesting to see than listening to Ava go on and on about Brody and Rod Galven's sibling rivalry. She had three of them. She'd seen it all when it came to brotherly spats.

When Ava moved her focus to Cole Forester, Jonas's best friend and fellow cattle rancher, Crys noticed a change in Jonas. He became increasingly fidgety and spent more time staring at his beer label than at his precious Ava.

With a gleam in her eye and a spark of creativity in her alcohol-pickled brain, Ava suddenly held up her hand like a Southern Baptist minister in the middle of a dynamic sermon. "I've got it! We should set you up with Cole!"

Immediately, Jonas sat up in his chair. "No."

Ava's eyes grew big as she set down her wineglass and pleaded her case. "Yes, Jonas! It's perfect."

"Ava, no."

"Think about it. Crys is single…"

"No."

"Cole's single…"

"No," Jonas said louder.

"They both enjoy the outdoors…"

"And long walks on the beach," Jonas sarcastically chimed in. "What are you, eHarmony? Seriously, Ava, listen to yourself. This is Cole we're talking about. You regularly call him a hermit, and for good reason. You know he doesn't socialize outside his comfort zone."

Crys sat in silence, listening to Jonas and Ava argue about whether or not Cole was a good match for her. At no time during the evening did she give any indication that she was even looking to date. By the exuberance in their discussion, she doubted either of them would stop to ask for her opinion on the matter anyway. It was almost like she wasn't even in the room.

"Ava, you know Cole's not going to go for it."

"We'll never know unless we try," Ava contended.

Jonas shook his head vigorously. "Uh-uh, there's no

'we' in this scheme of yours. Leave me out of it, Trick."

Crys smiled. She almost forgot about the nickname Jonas used to call Ava moments after they'd met. She loved that he still used it.

"Fine. I'll set them up myself."

With a break in the conversation, Crys waved her hand. "Hello? Do I get a say in this?"

Both turned to look at her. Jonas said "yes" and Ava said "no" simultaneously.

Crys laughed. "You two are so adorable."

Jonas quirked an eyebrow, and Ava smiled with pride, oblivious to Crys's goal of mollifying the situation. It was apparent that the small bit of alcohol she'd consumed had gone to her head.

Crys set her half-full glass of wine on the coffee table and took Ava's hands in hers. "Ava. I appreciate you wanting to introduce me to Jonas's friend, but…."

"But…"

Crys had hoped Ava would've already deduced the conclusion without her having to explain further. Jonas stood, as if he felt Crys's pain, and headed to the kitchen for another beer. She sighed and tried to explain her reservations about being set up. "I'm sure Cole is a great guy, but from what I'm gathering, he's not exactly a guy who's comfortable meeting new people."

"He thinks that, only because he's not met the right woman. You…" Ava drew out, "could be the right woman for him."

"Ava, honey?" Jonas said as he returned with two cold beers and handed one to Crys. "Maybe she doesn't want to be the right woman for Cole. Maybe she'd rather be the *wrong one.*" He wagged his brows and grinned, putting subliminal emphasis on his final two words.

Ava rolled her eyes. "Jonas, I don't even know what that means."

He chuckled and plopped back down in his chair. "You would if you hadn't drunk so much wine."

Ava swiveled her body on the couch to face her fiancé. "I'm not drunk, I'm just excited. I mean, this could really be good for her. Not to mention Cole." Ava turned her attention back to Crys. "This might be the reason to stay in Meeteetse."

Crys sank into the couch and drew her first refreshing sip of beer.

At least Jonas gets me.

Her second sip was even longer.

How was she going convince Ava that she didn't want a man to be the deciding factor in her search for a new home? If anything, men were the very reason she'd escaped Houston in the first place.

"Look," Ava bargained one last time. "It'll just be a casual evening. No pressure. I swear."

"Ha!" Jonas let out. "No pressure. Right."

"I'm serious," Ava asserted. "You know me, Crys. You know I'd never force you to do something you didn't want to do. But if you're interested in meeting a *very* handsome man"—Jonas coughed at that descriptor—"who has the same hard work ethic as yourself, why not take a chance? I'll invite him over for dinner and drinks tomorrow, and that's it. From there, we'll let nature take its course."

"A course inevitably heading toward derailment," Jonas added.

Ava ignored him. "What do you think? Are you game?"

A cloud of dread hovered over Crys as she pondered Ava's proposition. Inside, she begged to question why Jonas believed this idea was a surefire train wreck. Was the guy that bad? Was he such a recluse that even his best friend wouldn't go to bat for him?

Oh God, this is a bad idea. I just know it.

Chapter Six

Crys stared down into her bottle of beer. Every part of her pleaded to refuse. Cole Forester, according to Jonas, was an introvert, incapable of stepping out of his comfort zone. According to Ava, he was a hermit.

He sounded like a real winner.

The only thing he seemed to have going for him was his very sociable dog and his exceptional good looks. She guessed that was God's way of leveling the playing field for the poor fellow.

The more she thought about it, the more she came to realize Cole could not have been the same cowboy hottie she'd seen this afternoon. While the cowboy was good looking, he was also very confident and bold. Hardly the traits of this Cole fellow.

It was just as well they weren't the same, because if they were, meeting Cole formally tomorrow would be extremely awkward for both of them. Especially since she'd held that man at gunpoint.

"Can I sleep on it?" Crys finally asked, hoping to take the pressure off for a little while.

"I think that's a great idea," Jonas said, slamming his empty bottle on the coffee table. He stood and approached Ava, wrapping his arms around her from behind. "Let's give Crys a little breathing space, okay? Remember, she just got here. We don't want to give her a reason to leave first thing in the morning, right?"

"Yeah, you're right." Ava's enthusiasm sank, and she flashed her puppy-dog eyes at Crys. "I'm sorry. I didn't mean to be pushy."

"You weren't. You were cute."

"She's always cute," Jonas said, pulling her from the couch to a standing position. Like Fred Astaire, he spun her around ever so gallantly and gazed at her in awe before he planted a soft kiss on her forehead. "How about you get ready for bed, and I'll walk Crys down to her trailer."

"I am kind of tired all of a sudden," Ava admitted. "You sure you don't mind?"

"Not at all. Besides, I probably need to check and make sure you gals hooked up the electric properly. It gets cold up here in the mountains."

Ava swatted his arm, and Crys threw her bottle cap at him. "You know better than that, you chauvinistic pig."

Jonas's whole face lit up in a toothy grin. "I'm just

kidding, ladies." He led Ava to their bedroom and kissed her good night in the doorway.

Crys turned away as it was hardly a quick peck and finished the last of her beer. She looked up the minute it was safe to do so, and waved good night to Ava. "Thanks again for dinner."

"You are so welcome, Crys. Good night."

Jonas closed the bedroom door and sighed. "You ready for bed too, or would you like another beer?"

"Nah, I'm good." As she stood, she noticed the table full of dirty dishes, but Jonas assured her he'd take care of them. "You sure? We can get this all cleaned up in no time."

"Don't worry about it. I got it."

Crys made her way to the kitchen to throw away her empty beer bottle and met Jonas at the door. After tugging on her boots and jacket, she walked with him to the barn in silence with the subject of Cole tagging close behind. She could even feel its presence while they topped off all the stalled horses' water buckets.

As they stopped at Jericho's and filled his, Crys couldn't take it anymore. She leaned against the stall and spat the one question she was dying to know.

"So, what's wrong with this friend of yours?"

Jonas gave her a sideways glance and huffed. "Wrong

with him? Nothing, as far as I'm concerned."

Crys rolled her eyes. "Seriously, Jonas. Spill it. What's the real reason why I shouldn't meet Cole? Is he not my type or something?"

"I don't know you well enough to know your type."

He shut off the water and rolled up the hose. A tactic for beating around the bush, Crys guessed. She was not about to let him get away with it. "Okay, so I'm not *his* type?"

Jonas laughed. "Can't say that either. In fact, you're exactly the kind of woman he'd go for."

"But…"

"But Cole wouldn't date you even if he wanted to." Jonas looked at her as if he hoped his vague explanation would be enough to satisfy her curiosity. Crys returned a gesture that said otherwise.

"Look," he finally said, scratching the scruff on his jaw. "Cole's a peculiar kind of guy. Not your run-of-the-mill cowboy."

"Well, that's a start. And quite possibly the best thing I've heard about him all night."

"While that may be true, he's also stubborn as a mule."

"What man isn't?" Crys countered.

"What I'm trying to say is…he has rules. When it comes to dating and women."

Crys couldn't help but smile. The more Jonas delayed the issue, the more intriguing Cole became. "This oughta be good."

Jonas leaned against the stall and crossed his ankles. "The rule is he won't date anyone who is either a friend or family member of his own friends. Meaning, if we know you, you're off-limits. He's lived by that rule for as long as I can remember, and he never breaks it. It's a good rule to have, I'd imagine. It keeps the conflict at bay and the drama away. And trust me, Cole's all about a drama-free life."

"I can appreciate that. I'm an advocate for drama-free too. That's why I left Houston. To find a quiet place to call home without the fuss of someone else trying to run my life. I'm done with that."

Jonas's gaze fell to his boots in guilt. "I'm sorry Ava's not allowing that for you."

Crys waved it off. "She's fine. She and I go way back."

"Yeah, but this is a whole new side of her, even for me. She's not normally like this. I don't know, maybe it's the wine. Maybe it's her motherly instinct kicking in. Either way, I know it's not her intention to be overbearing. She's just really happy you're here. I know she's missed you."

A smile tugged at Crys's lips. She had missed Ava too. Seeing her after all these years was Crys's incentive for checking out Meeteetse. If it weren't for Ava, she'd have already bought a place in Big Horn.

"Anyway," Jonas said, pushing away from the stall, "when it comes to Cole, I know he's not going to be up for this whole blind date thing. I'm only telling you this because I'd hate for you to get your hopes up. When he turns Ava down, it's nothing personal toward you."

****

"He said yes!"

Crys bolted upright in her bed, smacking her head on the ceiling of her trailer. Before she could get her bearings, Ava squealed at the top of her lungs and leapt inside.

"He said yes! Isn't this great?"

Crys rubbed her head, glaring at Ava. She wasn't much of a morning person. Top that off with waking up to Ava screaming, and she wasn't much of an Ava person right now.

As she tried to collect her wits through the smarting of the pain, she gathered nothing but confusion. "What are you talking about?"

Ava approached Crys with wide eyes and an animated smile, both of which scared the heck out of her. "Cole. I called him this morning about meeting you, and he said YES!"

Crys drew back. The last thing she remembered before she fell asleep last night was the conversation she and Jonas had about Cole and his rule about never dating friends of friends. "He actually agreed to it?"

"I know, right? It's so not like him, but—"

"But, wait," Crys interrupted. "What did you say to him?"

Ava brought her forearms up and stacked them on Crys's mattress, resting her chin on top. "I asked him if he'd like to come over for dinner tonight, and he hemmed and hawed a little…"

"Ava…"

"Okay, a lot, but he still finally agreed."

Crys fixed her gaze on Ava. "What were his exact words?"

Ava bit her lip and cringed. "He said, 'Fine, whatever it takes for you to stop badgering me.' But that's still a yes."

Ava's excitement was painful to see. After last night, Crys had no problem keeping her expectations low when it came to Cole. If anything, she was glad he had rules about dating. She should've had one of her own: beware the friend who insists on playing matchmaker.

Crys fell backward onto her pillow and groaned. "I'm going to regret this, aren't I?"

"Maybe," Ava said, tugging on her arm. "Or you can

do what my friend Rhonda says. Take the bull by the horns and ride him for eight seconds."

Ava glanced upward, saying the phrase over again in her head. "Wait, I don't think that sounds right for what I meant."

Crys burst out laughing. "Oh, I don't know. I think Rhonda's warped version of the phrase sounds more appealing. When do I get to meet *her*?"

"Monday." Ava smiled. "You'll like her."

Crys couldn't get the image of riding some sexy, rowdy cowboy for a swift eight seconds out of her head once Ava had put it there. "I *already* like her."

Chapter Seven

Cole pounded his fist on the hood of his truck.

What the hell was he thinking?

He should've said no to Ava's invite. He should've reminded her about his rule, and told her to stick her matchmaking plans up Jonas's butt, because he knew darn well Jonas had something to do with it.

Of all people, Jonas knew exactly where he stood when it came to certain women—even sexy-as-sin blonde barrel racers like Crys. He wasn't much for dating to begin with. One night stands, yes. But wining, dining, and making boring small talk was not in his gamut of relationship strategies.

In the interest of getting laid, he could never even think of doing that with someone Ava cared about. It was so wrong, on so many levels. The result of a potential bad experience alone ran the risk of tension, ill feelings, and disappointment, all of which he dreaded to put between him and his best friend's fiancée. Worse even, his best friend.

As happy as he'd made Ava by saying yes, he felt miserable. His stomach balled in knots, and a sour taste filled his mouth as he imagined Crys's reaction to seeing him again. He wondered if she had told Jonas and Ava about their initial encounter on the highway yesterday. Even if she hadn't, he knew no good would come from meeting the cute little hellcat for dinner.

On the bright side, if he went through with it today, the whole holding-him-at-gunpoint fiasco would be brought out in the open amongst the four of them, instead of on Monday when Brody and Rod Galven showed up for work. With those two, a whole slew of jokes were sure to arise.

Cole looked at Sammy, who sat patiently at his feet. "What are you looking at?"

Sammy barked once, as if to say, *An idiot.*

"I know, I *am* an idiot," he replied, squatting down to pat Sammy's head. "But did you see her? She's beautiful. She's an angel. A beautiful…angelic…mistake."

Sammy let out a rolling pleasure growl and offered his paw. Cole accepted and shook his head. "Don't worry. I'll let her down softly. But you, mister, better stay clear of her too. I saw how you kissed up to her yesterday."

As if trying to apologize, Sammy lay down on the

ground and rolled in submission.

"You're not sorry, Sam. I know you. You'll do it again tomorrow." Cole scrubbed his companion's belly, recalling how gorgeous Crys had looked when she bent to pet him. "I don't blame you. She's one tough chick to ignore. If I thought she'd be receptive to it, I'd pal around her legs just so she'd scratch me behind the ears too."

Cole stood and tried to put her out of his mind. After a few agonizing moments of failure, he looked down at Sammy, who had obediently sat up and waited his command. He looked his dog dead in the eye and said, "We're doomed."

****

While Ava spent all day cooking in the house, Crys helped Jonas turn the horses out and grain the herd of pregnant cows grazing in the nearby pasture. She was glad Ava hadn't asked her to help with the preparations for tonight's dinner, because she'd be about as much help as a toddler.

Growing up in a house full of males, Crys had never hung back with her mother to learn the skills of cooking and cleaning. Ladies work, as her father liked to call it, was the last thing she wanted to do when there was more enticing fun to be had tending horses and watching her brothers train for competitions. Even after her mother grew sick when Crys was a teen, her father never encouraged her to fill those shoes. It wasn't until after her mother died that he had hired a maid and an occasional cook.

Regardless of her unusual upbringing, she'd always preferred to work outside. Nothing made the time pass more quickly than vigorous, physical labor in the open air. And no place she'd ever been to was more open and refreshing than Wyoming.

Between filling and carrying two dozen buckets of crushed corn and minerals, mucking close to thirty horse stalls, and running the John Deere to scrape dark, sloppy manure from the cow lot, the day flew by. And working alongside Jonas also provided additional benefits. She learned that not all men were pushy and inconsiderate.

All her life, she'd been pressed to carry more than her weight in order to keep up with her older brothers. If she failed, she was sure to collect backlash. With Jonas, even though she still outperformed most females twice her size, he came to her rescue whenever she showed the slightest bit of struggle.

Graciousness was not a familiar trait among the men she'd previously known, and it would take a great while before she got used to it. She could barely wrap her head around a male stranger pulling over to assist her without a depraved ulterior motive.

Ever since she'd arrived at the McKinley ranch, she felt a pang of guilt for her rash behavior toward the gentleman in the black Stetson hat. And ever since she saw the silver GMC in Jonas's driveway, the possibility that he and Cole Forester were one and the same nagged at her as well.

While she was eager to know for sure, she dreaded to find out the truth. What if Cole *was* the cowboy in the silver truck? How would he react when he saw her again? Would he hold it against her? Would he stick around, or make a scene storming out?

Oh God.

She felt sick. Very sick. Maybe if she played that up beforehand, she could postpone meeting Cole for another day. As she gathered a change of clothes from her trailer and traipsed up the porch steps with Jonas, she seriously considered it—until she walked through the door.

The smell of something sweet baking in the oven smacked her in the face. Off the kitchen, a warm glow of red taper candles lit a table set for four. Each place setting gleamed with elegant white china, shiny silverware, and fancy red swan napkins.

No way could she fake an illness now. After all the

work Ava had done, it would be plain rude. Instead, she faked a smile.

"Uh, honey?" Jonas called out. "I thought you said this would be casual?"

Ava came around the corner of the kitchen with a mixing bowl and a wooden spoon, stirring what looked like warm chocolate sauce. Her beautiful smile prefaced her explanation. "It's still casual...with just a hint of sophistication."

Jonas toed off his boots and hung up his hat and coat, staring at Ava as though she had three heads. "We're not entertaining the queen of England, you know. It's Cole." He thumbed between him and Crys. "And a couple of sweaty cowhands."

Ava approached him and stood on tiptoes to plop a kiss on his lips. "Even sweaty cowhands deserve a nice meal with all the trimmings."

"Yeah, well, that's going to make Cole tuck tail and run."

"Not when he finds out I've made his favorite. Cajun-marinated steaks and twice-baked potatoes with cheese and bacon."

Jonas leaned in for another kiss. "What about Crys? If you've not noticed, she's looking to jet out of here too."

Ava shot Crys a sideways glance. "Don't worry. I've

made her favorite as well. Cheesecake drizzled with homemade chocolate sauce."

"Aw, you remembered." Crys removed her jacket and hung it up next to Jonas's. "But really, Ava. This is all too much. You shouldn't have done this."

"I wanted to. You have no idea how happy I am that you're considering Meeteetse as your home. If anything, I'm hoping to convince you that Wyoming has all you're looking for."

Crys bit her lip. That niggling guilt she'd been feeling since she arrived welled up again.

"What's wrong?" Ava asked. "Did I say something I shouldn't have?"

"No, you're fine. I'm just trying to get used to everyone being so helpful and accommodating." She looked between Jonas and Ava, who were now gazing at her with uncertainty. "What I mean is, I've never known people to do so much for others. I haven't even been here twenty-four hours and you've done more than I deserve. Ava, you went out of your way to pick me up and haul my trailer in. You've cooked two amazing meals... Even Jonas went above and beyond by carrying the last two buckets of feed for me this afternoon when I almost tripped.

"Where I come from, I've always had to prove myself. Work twice as hard and make sure someone didn't take advantage of me. All those things have been ground into my head since I was strong enough to throw a hay bale. I come from the big city of Houston, and it's completely different from here. Don't get me wrong, Houston is great. I've got nothing against it. But here...in Wyoming...it's a whole new way of thinking. Everyone's so laid back and gracious. So gracious, I almost feel guilty."

Ava reached for Crys and touched her arm. "You've got nothing to feel guilty about."

"Yeah, well what about the fact that I drew my shotgun on a guy who'd pulled over to help me yesterday when I was broke down?"

Jonas's and Ava's eyes widened at the same time. "You what?"

"You heard me. I held some dude at gunpoint and told him to move on, because, in my twisted mind, he was there to take advantage of me. When in reality, he was probably just trying to be a Good Samaritan."

Jonas took a step back from her and raised his hands. "Remind me never to tick you off."

"Jonas," Ava scolded.

"He's right, Ava. There was no reason for me to get all defensive with the guy. He was nothing but a perfect gentleman, and I overreacted."

"Yeah, but you didn't know that at the time," Ava tried

to reason.

"Regardless," Crys argued, "I didn't give him a chance."

"Sadly, in this day and age, you can't. We, as women, *have to* second-guess a stranger who comes to our aid. Those that don't, end up on the evening news."

"I have to agree with Ava," Jonas said, crossing his arms. "You were a lone woman out in the middle of nowhere. You did what you thought you had to do to protect yourself. You can't beat yourself up for that. But from now on, remember that you're surrounded by friends who care about you, and are completely willing to lend a hand…even if some of them go a little overboard."

Ava elbowed Jonas and frowned. "Yes, what Jonas said, but without so much emphasis on the last part."

Jonas gathered her up in his arms, mixing bowl and all, and hugged her close. "Admit it. You went way overboard here with this casual dinner."

Ava giggled under his tickling hands and squirmed away. "Careful, Jonas, I'm armed," she warned, holding up the chocolate-covered wooden spoon.

He ignored her threat and swatted her behind. "Why don't you bring some of that into the bedroom tonight?"

Ava took one look at her spoon. "The chocolate sauce?"

"I meant your feistiness, Trick. But that'll do too."

"Get your shower," Ava commanded, shaking her head. She eyed Jonas as he strolled into their bedroom and shut the door, and only then did she focus on Crys. When she saw that Crys had brought a change of clothes, she smiled. "You better hurry and get your shower too. Cole should be here soon."

Chapter Eight

Cole pulled up to the barn at the McKinley ranch and killed the engine. Pure dread clung tight around him, making the muscles in his back and shoulders tense.

Relax…it's just a casual dinner with friends.

He groaned and hung his head. *So doomed.*

Sammy whined in sympathy and nuzzled next to him. Cole dropped his hand from the steering wheel and patted his dog's side.

"All right, let's get this over with."

He opened the truck door and stepped out, with Sammy leaping to the ground right behind him. Without waiting, the dog took off running for the front porch.

"Traitor," Cole mumbled as he took his precious time walking to the house.

Sammy barked three times once he made it to the porch and sat obediently. He wagged his tail back and forth across the floorboards, anxious for someone to open the door. By the time Cole had reached the steps, Jonas greeted him with a crooked smile and a beer.

Judging by the look on his friend's face, Cole figured that the casual dinner date Ava had promised had gone awry. "Bribing me now?"

Jonas lifted his own bottle to his lips. "If that's what it takes to keep you here."

Cole accepted the beer and looked beyond Jonas at the formal candlelight dinner awaiting him. "Great." He sighed and chugged his beer until it was empty.

Jonas gave Cole's shoulder a sound pat. "It's just dinner. No one's asking you to date anyone."

"It's kind of implied with the whole candles and shit."

"I know, I know. Ava went hog-wild, but you gotta go through with this. If you don't, you know it'll hurt her feelings. Look at all the trouble she went to."

Cole narrowed his eyes, trying to decode his friend's angle. Jonas knew Cole's rule, and yet he still supported Ava and her grand scheme instead of talking her out of it. That bothered him more than anything. Add to the fact that he and Crys had already met on the highway in a relatively intense manner, and this was bound to be the worst night of his life. Assuming she hadn't put two and two together after seeing his truck at the McKinley ranch yesterday, Crys was certainly in for a shock. Come to think of it, her reaction might be the only highlight of his evening. "I suppose I'll stay. But I'm going to need another beer."

"That's the spirit, buddy."

Jonas stepped aside, and Cole and Sammy entered the living room. Immediately, Cole took off his cowboy hat and looked around. Ava met him with a big grin as she carried a platter of heaping potatoes and set it on the kitchen table.

"Well, hello there, Cole. How are you this fine evening?"

Upon hearing Ava's loaded question, Cole's first inclination was to grumble in complaint. But before he could let it fly, Jonas nudged him in the back. "I'm great. Thanks."

"I made your favorite," Ava enticed him.

He glanced at the sizzling steaks in the middle of the table. "I see that."

"Well, come on in and take a seat. I'll let Crys know you're here."

Cole and Jonas exchanged looks, whereupon Cole grimaced and Jonas offered a simple smile.

Still in apprehension, he removed his coat and hung it up with his hat. He watched Jonas as he made his way to the kitchen, and toed off his own boots. When he reached the elaborately decorated table, Jonas joined him with a fresh cold one.

"How about you nurse this one," Jonas joked.

Cole took the beer and forced himself to sip it. "Happy?" He waited for Jonas to choose a seat so that he could take the spot next to him, putting both the women on the opposite side of the table. If nothing else was going to be his decision tonight, then he'd at least choose where he sat.

By the time he situated himself at the side of the table against the wall, Sammy found a spot on the floor next to him and lay down. Ava came around the corner and joined them. "She'll just be a few."

Cole gripped his beer and stared in the direction of the hallway. Although he'd much rather skip out on the dinner before Crys made an appearance, the anticipation of seeing the look on her face the second she laid eyes on him held him riveted to the chair.

In the passing minutes he spent waiting, Ava and Jonas made small talk, which might or might not have included him. He tried to listen, tried to follow their conversation about God knows what, but he couldn't focus on anything save for Crys's grand entrance.

When he heard the bathroom door open, his heart kicked into high gear. Sammy leapt to his feet and met her as she walked into the living room. She wore another pair of tight blue jeans, and a blue plaid flannel shirt that matched her eyes. Her long hair was loosely braided this time and brought to the front, innocently drawing attention to her buxom chest. Simply put, she stole his breath away.

"Here she is," Ava announced, turning around in her chair. "Cole, this is my dear friend Crys Willingham. Crys, this is Cole."

Crys looked up from Sammy and stopped petting him with a deer-in-the-headlights look on her face. Cole stood up from the table out of politeness and smiled. "It's a pleasure to meet you, Crys."

"Oh my God, it *is* you."

Cole heard the shakiness in her voice and reveled in it. The brave and confident woman he'd met on the highway had vanished. For the first time since they'd met, she seemed approachable.

Ava looked between the two of them, confused. "Wait. You two know each other?"

"Informally, we've already met," Cole explained. "But the last time she saw me, I was on the receiving end of her Remington."

Jonas choked on his beer, coughing and laughing at the same time. "Cole's the guy you pulled a gun on yesterday?"

Crys cringed. "I'm afraid so."

Jonas beat his chest to clear his airway. "This is classic hilarious! I love it! You have no idea how this makes my day!"

Ava frowned at Jonas. "Get ahold of yourself, Jonas. This is *not* funny."

"Yes, it is." He pointed at Crys. "You know you're on the verge of laughter. I mean seriously, what are the chances that the one guy you pull a gun on is the same guy Ava's trying to fix you up with."

Ava glared at Jonas now. "I'm not fixing them up." With a panicked expression, she turned to Cole. "I wasn't. I just thought it would be nice for you two to meet, and whatever happened afterward—"

"It's fine," Cole said, trying to comfort Ava. Even though he knew Ava had high hopes of matching them up, he didn't want her to feel responsible when things didn't work out.

And they wouldn't work out.

He still refused to date Crys, no matter how compatible they were.

"Cole," Crys said, taking a step forward. "I'm so sorry I did that to you. If I could relive that afternoon, I would've—"

"Checked your fluids sooner?"

Crys's mouth hung open for a few seconds, and then she laughed. "Yeah, I guess that would've been a good idea."

"All I want to know is, was the shotgun loaded?"

Cole saw Crys swallow hard. "Of-of course it was. It always is."

"Good. That makes me feel a whole lot better."

Crys furrowed her brow and stuffed her hands in the back pockets of her jeans. "Are you crazy?"

Cole crossed his arms. "Not at all. I have to admit I admired you from the moment I saw you. Then when you had the nerve to draw a weapon against me, I thought even more highly of you. Crazy would've been respecting you if you were too stupid to load it."

Jonas and Ava sat dumbfounded. But Crys smiled as if she appreciated his off-the-wall logic. If anything, he hoped he'd made her feel better about the whole situation so they could finally put it behind them.

He extended his hand toward the open seat across from him. "Now, why don't we forget about this whole fiasco and enjoy Ava's meal before it gets cold."

He heard Crys draw a long breath and let it out. "I'd like that."

Cole winked at Ava, who'd been sitting on pins and needles. By taking control and ironing out the kinks, he knew he gave her some reprieve. She deserved it, especially after spending the better part of her afternoon cooking for them.

"Thank you, Cole," Ava said in appreciation.

As Crys took her seat, Sammy followed and lay down beneath the table. Jonas burst into laughter again.

"I'm sorry, I can't stop picturing Cole at gunpoint. I wish I'd been there to see it!"

Cole faked a smile as he bit down. "Go on. Get it all out now, 'cause I'm telling you, you bring this up tomorrow when Rod's here, and I'll—"

"Ah, come on!" Jonas spat. "Don't make me hold this in."

"I'm serious, Jonas. Rod better not find out about this, or I'll kick your ass."

"Cole's right," Ava piped in. "Rod is the last person who needs to hear about this."

"Who's Rod?" Crys asked, looking a little worried.

"He's one of our hired hands," Ava explained. "Great guy, hard worker, but he loves to poke fun at his brother, Brody, and even Jonas every chance he gets."

"But not Cole?"

"He'd like to," Jonas said, "but strangely, Cole never gives him a reason. So this is perfect. For once, he'll be in the hot seat."

"I'm not afraid of the heat," Cole retorted. "I just don't think we need to throw Crys into the fire with me."

"I can take it," Crys said, sticking up for herself. "I

grew up with three pain-in-the-ass brothers. I think I can handle this Rod fellow."

"Don't be a hero," Jonas warned with a wry grin. "Rod'll make mincemeat out of ya. And afterward, he'll be the one you'd wish you could shoot. But don't. I need him this winter."

"Then it's settled," Ava stated as she threw her fiancé a look. "Not another word about this."

Jonas sighed in disappointment. "You're no fun."

After Jonas swore to silence, he folded his hands and said grace. From then on, polite conversation opened on the subject of the prepared meal as they passed it around the table.

Ava informed Crys that Cajun steaks and twice-baked potatoes were Cole's favorite, although he couldn't understand why Crys needed to know that. It wasn't like they would ever be having dinner together in the future. This was a one-time deal, an exception he made to appease Ava, nothing more.

After that, Jonas made some joke that Ava hadn't made his favorite meal in quite a while. She, of course, dished back that Jonas hadn't done much to deserve it. A few moments of playful teasing bounced back and forth between them, and then they leaned across the table and kissed.

Cole and Crys exchanged mild looks of disgust and went back to eating. As hard as he tried, he couldn't keep from imagining a kiss with Crys. Not just a friendly peck, but a slow, tentative first kiss. He envisioned how her lips would feel against his own. How good she'd taste when he parted her lips.

"Don't you think so, Cole?" Ava asked.

Cole looked around and realized he'd zoned out, missing the whole conversation. "Think what?"

"Have you even been listening?"

He saw the grin Crys failed to hide as she glanced down at her plate.

Damn, she's cute.

"Earth to Cole," Ava interrupted again.

"I'm sorry. What did you ask me?"

"I asked you what you thought about Crys working on the ranch while she's here. We could really use her on the payroll since the female staff starts fall semester next week." Ava turned to Crys, explaining how Madeline, Jolee, Addison, and Hayden only worked full-time during the summer months when they were off from college.

As the two women discussed the ins and outs of the job offered to Crys, Cole pondered the possibilities himself.

If Crys agreed, he couldn't exactly avoid her. She'd be held to a ten-hour day like the other hired hands, working up a sweat on that beautiful body of hers. As much as he longed to see her muscles flex, working that close with her would be sheer agony.

Say no. Say no.

"I *could* use the extra money," Crys said aloud as she mulled it over. "Are you sure you have enough work for me? I don't want a pity job."

"There's enough work for two of you," Jonas said, elbowing Cole. "Ain't that right?"

Cole hated the position Jonas had put him in. With one sentence, he could encourage Crys to stick around or trigger her to move on—the latter one making him look like a jerk.

"Maybe she doesn't want the work. I mean, maybe she'll be too busy looking at property." He eyed Crys, who seemed to hang on his every word. "I assume that's why you're here. Right?"

"It is."

Though he fought it, Crys captured his gaze. She was the most beautiful woman he'd ever seen. And as much as he wanted to give in, he couldn't.

She was Ava's friend.

Untouchable.

The fact that she represented everything forbidden to him only made him want her that much more.

With her looking to him for reassurance, he knew she'd be better off making this decision without his influence.

"This is all you, Crys. Not me, Ava, or Jonas. Just you."

She wiped the corner of her mouth with her napkin and finally looked away. "The only plans I had were finding a place to call home. Whether that be here or Big Horn."

"Big Horn's nice," Cole interjected before he could stop himself.

"Yes, but so is Meeteetse," Ava added. "Plus, if you found a farm here, you'd already have a full-time job lined up for making those payments. Not to mention friends who'd be close by to help you settle in. Big Horn's beautiful, but it would be quite a commute on the weekends just to see you."

"True…"

Cole grabbed his beer and lifted it to his lips, staring at the ceiling. *Decide already, will ya?*

"All right, fine. I'll take the job, but let's leave the duration open in case I find property outside of Meeteetse. Fair enough?"

Cole downed his beer, his emotions running all over the place. He was racked with both aggravation and nervous excitement. But despite what he felt, he wasn't going to give in and break his rule. Crys Willingham was as good as trouble and a complication he didn't need in his perfectly functional bachelor's life.

Chapter Nine

All through dinner, Crys noticed that Cole was in his own little world. It all seemed to stem from the moment she'd accepted a job on the McKinley ranch. Even when everyone was laughing about the blunders she and Ava had experienced from their earlier rodeo days, he hardly smiled or joined in the conversation. She'd hoped he'd have settled in and shared something by the time Ava served dessert, but no such luck. The only thing she learned about him was his preference for Budweiser.

When the guys grabbed a couple more beers from the fridge and left with Sammy to sit out on the porch, she asked Ava about his quiet reserve while they did the dishes. Ava assured her that Cole was just being Cole, and unfortunately, he wasn't a man of many words.

"Give it time. He'll open up once he gets to know you."

That was the problem. Crys didn't know if she wanted Cole to get to know her. She recently made a promise to herself that she'd start her life anew without a man's interference. Yet here she was fussing over some guy who clearly waged his own battles.

She shouldn't care that Cole had some bizarre rule about not dating her, or that he clammed up for no good reason. And she certainly shouldn't want to push the issue when the whole thing might explode in her face. Hadn't past experience taught her anything?

No matter how much she tried to convince herself that Cole wasn't someone she should concern herself with, her heart begged otherwise. Ever since she'd locked him in her steel sights, she couldn't shake him. She'd gotten a long hard look at his handsome face, and she wished she could've reached out and touched it. What she liked about him most was that he didn't flaunt his exceptional good looks like the other cocky cowboys she'd known. She wondered if Cole even knew how sexy he was.

His taut, muscular build was his most noticeable asset, but the components of his gorgeous face were what set him apart.

Like the sun, his chocolate-brown eyes held a warmth both alluring and dangerous. Beneath their soft, inviting color, she saw a man full of reckless desire, capable of roping any woman he wanted. His smile, on the few occasions he shared it, was a shroud for the wicked rascal within. And oh, what she wouldn't give to know that part of him. If only he didn't have that so-called rule.

Before she found herself drawn to him even more, she decided she'd better skip out while he was preoccupied with Jonas on the porch. It would make saying good-bye that much easier.

"I think I'm going to call it a night, Ava."

"Well, I hope you enjoyed your evening." Ava looked far too hopeful.

"Yes, it was very nice. And the dinner you made was fantastic. You sure know your way around a kitchen."

"I learned a few good dishes over the years," Ava said, hugging Crys good night. "It's nice to have someone else to cook for besides Jonas. It always feels like such a waste to cook for two."

"I wouldn't know," Crys confessed.

"Well, you never can tell… Things might work out between you and…" Ava gestured in the direction of the porch, "some eligible bachelor."

"Don't hold your breath. Besides, I'm not so sure he's my type."

"Uh, let's see… Cowboy. Tall. Dark. Handsome." Ava ticked each one off on her fingertips. "Which one of those *is not* your type? If I recall, those very traits used to be your staple."

"Shut up." Crys shook her head, unable to deny her rebellious past. With the strict upbringing she had to live under, who could blame her.

At the door, Crys slid on her boots and righted her hat on her head. When she reached for her coat, she couldn't help but notice Cole's hanging next to hers. She found herself taking a whiff of hers as she slung it around her shoulders, wondering if Cole's scent had transferred onto the fabric of her Carhartt.

Just as she thought she might have smelled him, Ava poked her head out the door and let Jonas know she was going to bed.

"I'm right behind you, Trick."

Before Crys could step out onto the porch, Jonas shuffled Ava through the door, his hands on her hips. "See you in the morning, Crys. Night, Cole!"

Her friends left her standing at the door.

Alone.

With Cole—and his dog.

Sammy now sat in front of her, wagging his tail. Cole remained seated in his rocking chair, looking about as uncomfortable as she felt.

After giving his dog some affection, Crys stiffened her back, and found her courage. She grabbed Cole's coat from the hook and brought it out to him. "It's getting kind of chilly tonight."

"Always does in the valley," he drawled out, slipping it on.

"Mind if I sit with you?"

Instead of answering, he picked up a full beer, popped it open, and handed it to her. Crys accepted, a little unnerved by his continual low-key façade, and plopped herself into the rocking chair beside him. She couldn't take his ridiculous behavior any longer.

"All right, Cole. I have to know. Why are you so upset with me taking this job?"

"I'm not upset."

"You're not?"

"Nope."

"Okay, then why won't you talk to me?"

He scrunched his brow in confusion. "I *am* talking to you."

Crys sighed. "In the literal sense you are, but it's not without reservation. Why is that?"

"I don't know."

"You *do* know," she fired back. "You're just not saying."

As if sensing the tension between them, Sammy placed his head in Crys's lap. Absently, she petted him until another reason occurred to her. "Is it because your dog is more fond of me than you are?"

Cole snickered. "No."

"Is it because I could've shot you? I mean let's be realistic. I had no intention of pulling the trigger on you, and you know it. Besides, I had the safety on."

"Like I told you earlier, I was not put off by your need to protect yourself."

Crys let her raised hand slap her leg in exasperation. "Okay, so then what is it? What is your beef with me?"

"You really want to know?"

"Yes, I do. Especially if I'm going to be working with you day after day."

"All right, I'll tell you. But you're not going to like it, I assure you."

"How about you let me be the judge of that."

Cole took a long drink and set his empty bottle down on the small table between them. He swiveled his body to face her and looked her dead in the eye. "Every time I see you, all I want to do is take you into my arms and kiss you. It's an itch I can't scratch. And what makes it worse is that no matter how hard I try to get you out of my mind, how hard I *fight* to keep you out of my head, you're there anyway.

"And the kicker is...I don't really want you there. I'm a bachelor because I choose to be, and with you waltzing in here with your GMC Denali and Remington shotgun, not to mention your rockin' body, you're complicating the hell out of my life. Everything about you is what I'd want in a woman—if I were looking. Which I'm not."

"Okay…" Crys wasn't sure if she was more surprised by his words or the fact that he said more in that moment than he had all night.

"But you know what? None of this matters. It doesn't matter that I've thought extensively about us hunting together, or us horseback riding across this farm. Or how amazing it would be to wake up to the sight of your beautiful face one fine morning. None of it matters because it can never happen. I want you, Crys Willingham, like no man has ever wanted you, and I can't have you."

A loud noise erupted on the other side of the window behind them, followed by muffled voices. Cole exhaled heavily and sank back into his rocking chair.

It was apparent that either Ava or Jonas—or, no doubt, both of them—had been eavesdropping on their conversation and couldn't help but react to Cole's unexpected confession.

Like her nosy friends, Crys hadn't seen that coming either.

Chapter Ten

Cole's words echoed around her.

"I want you, Crys Willingham, like no man has ever wanted you, and I can't have you."

Inside, she was just as distressed as he was. Though her heart warmed to the idea of Cole desiring her that much, she wasn't ready for anything serious. Admittedly, she could say she felt a serious attraction to him too, but given his irritation level, he'd probably not want to hear it. Nonetheless, something had to be said. What, exactly, was lost to her.

Instead of trying to find the right words, she thought maybe a little consolation might help. She reached out to touch his hand, but he jerked it away and stood. Sammy jumped to his feet as well, panting with excitement. Cole's face was rendered emotionless.

"It's late. I'll walk you to your horse trailer."

Crys looked down at the full beer in her hand, not wanting the night to end on a negative note. She had so many unanswered questions and no knowledge of how to go about asking them without adding more tension. Lord knew they had enough friction between them already, as it seemed she'd wreaked more havoc in his life in two days than he could deal with.

Reluctant to upset him more, she pushed herself out of the rocking chair and stepped off the porch. Without another word, they walked together toward the barn, Sammy close on Cole's heels. In the silence of their stroll, the distance from the house to her trailer felt longer than usual. Each step had her wishing she would've just said good night right after dinner and parted ways. She could've avoided this whole situation had she not sat down next to him on the porch.

Hindsight was always twenty-twenty, but it didn't make her feel any better.

When they reached the door of her horse trailer, he opened it for her like a gentleman. "Good night, Crys."

"Wait," Crys said, halting him by the arm. He glanced down at her hand and then back at her, as if the physical contact infuriated him. Immediately, she let go. "So that's it? You confess your deepest desires to me and walk away?"

"That's the intention."

"So, regardless of what you want, you're sticking to your *rule*."

His big brown eyes turned to slits. "Jonas told you about that?"

"Yes, he did. And like I told him yesterday, I respect your rule. I think it's great that you don't want to put any awkwardness between you and your friends. I don't want that either, and I'm sure as heck not looking for anything serious. But it's obvious there's some attraction between us."

She expected him to at least agree, but he neither spoke nor reacted. He just stood there, silent as the grave.

"Okay so, since you haven't denied it, I'm going to assume you *are* aware of my attraction toward you, but are still afraid to drive a wedge between you and your friends. So the way I see it, there'd only be awkwardness if they knew."

"What are you talking about?"

"Say, for instance, if you and I decided to see each other in secret, and we did all those things you talked about—hunting, horseback riding…who knows, I might even let you kiss me—the point is, if we did all that without anyone knowing, where's the awkwardness? Personally, I don't see any harm in testing the waters. And let's face it, it's a lot easier than trying to resist each other."

Cole crossed his arms and widened his stance. "Let me see if I follow you. We see each other without anyone necessarily knowing. And if things get too complicated, we split."

"Yeah. I believe it's called dating," Crys joked. "Again, with no plans of anything serious. Just a little fling while I'm in town."

Cole didn't look convinced.

She stepped forward. "You said yourself that you wanted me in a way no man has ever wanted me. So, why fight it?"

The space between them was but a few inches, close enough that she could hear every strenuous breath he took. As she watched his chest rise and fall, she dared to slip her hand inside his Carhartt and feel those muscles, warm and hard.

"What do you have to lose, cowboy?"

Crys saw his Adam's apple bob as he swallowed. "You certainly drive a hard bargain."

She swelled with pride knowing she might well have broken him. "So, what'll it be?"

He drew in a huge breath and let it fly. "Against my better judgement, I'll agree to this dangerous game of yours. On two conditions."

Her stomach fluttered with anticipation. "Name 'em."

"Total honesty. No head games, no lies. I hate that shit."

"Seems reasonable. And second?"

"We sleep on it. If in the morning we're both still willing…"

"Deal. But I've got a condition of my own."

"I'm listening."

"No matter what happens between us, we stay true to who we are. We don't do anything we aren't comfortable doing, and we don't say anything we don't mean. Don't butter me up with flattery or talk yourself up to a pedestal you can't reach for climbing. We are who we are, and we don't make excuses for it. You in?"

She stepped back and stuck out her hand. Cole glanced down and smirked. He seized her wrist and jerked her into his arms, causing her hat to flip off her head and tumble to the ground from the force of her body colliding with his.

"This isn't the kind of deal we shake on, darlin'." He dipped his head, and captured her lips in a deep, possessive, mind-blowing kiss.

All intelligible thoughts vanished save for those that pertained to the talented mouth and strong hands that held her captive. She'd never been kissed like this before, and quite frankly, she didn't think she would ever again.

Cole Forester had just ruined it for any man who might come after him.

****

Cole stood in awe of the woman he held in his arms. The beautiful angel he'd just kissed. Was he dreaming?

He couldn't be. He could still taste Crys on his lips, sweet like cheesecake with chocolate sauce and tart like the hops from her beer. It was an unexpected but pleasant combination on his palate.

Even more unexpected was the deal he'd just made with her. How could he be so weak?

As he stared into her soulful blue eyes, he knew sleeping on it wouldn't change how he felt now that he'd kissed her. Though she was still Ava's friend, and a woman he should resist, he had to see her again.

Her body felt so good against his. He imagined she'd be soft in all the right places and well-toned in all the rest.

"Are you going to stand here all night and stare at me? Or are we going to sleep on it…together."

Cole released her and stepped back. Her offer sounded far too enticing to his ears. "That wasn't the terms we agreed on."

"No, it wasn't."

He bent over and snatched up her Stetson, dusting it off before handing it back to her. If he didn't leave right now, he was going to do something he knew he'd regret.

Squaring his shoulders, he tipped his hat.

"Good night, Crys."

Chapter Eleven

Cole woke the next morning exhausted from a restless night's sleep. After their first kiss, he craved Crys every waking moment, dying for another.

He climbed off the couch, as that's where he ended up falling asleep, and tromped up the stairs to his bathroom, dreading the day he had ahead of him. Knowing how badly he wanted to kiss her again, the hours he'd spend working with her would only trickle by.

He considered taking another shower, a freezing cold one this time, but once he checked the time, he decided against it. Being late on the first day of working with Crys would only raise flags, and there was no way he'd give Jonas a reason to rile him.

As per their arrangement, everyone had to be kept in the dark in order to avoid any possible awkwardness, should he and Crys decide they didn't gel. It sounded good in theory, but he wondered how it would pan out once they started getting to know each other. As much as he didn't want it to affect his relationship with Jonas or Ava, Crys's feelings mattered to him as well.

The only consolation he had was that they agreed there'd be no lies between them. No matter what happened, they'd only keep the truth from everyone else.

As he dressed himself in front of the mirror, he wondered if that were even possible. Could he be one person around her and a different one around his friends?

On the drive there, he mulled it over in his head so intently that he barely remembered driving the entire distance from his place to Jonas's. As he pulled in, he glanced beside him, unsure if he even remembered to bring Sammy. To his relief, his loyal companion sat in the passenger seat, his head out the window.

Cole chuckled at the simplicity of dogs, wishing he could survive on an elementary approach to life. He used to live that way...until *Crys* showed up. Heaven help him, as much as he longed to be with her, he needed to keep his wits about him or this whole thing was going to backfire.

Shoving his truck into Park, he looked around for Crys. Maybe, after sleeping on it, she'd decided none of this was worth the risk, and he'd be off the hook.

He lifted his hat and ran his hand through his hair, blowing out a breath filled with anxiety. If this woman didn't kill him first, he'd be a total wreck by the time she was through with him. This whole acting like a puppet on a string had to end.

He stepped out of his truck and held the door open for Sammy. He watched his dog jump to the ground and run for the barn. The second Cole heard Crys's voice, he smiled. Even before he could see her, she made him react in ways no other woman had, and he couldn't stop it.

Walking in, he found Sammy right where he figured he'd be—at Crys's feet, receiving all kinds of affection. When she looked up, he felt as if the sun had risen again. Her eyes were that beautiful.

"Good morning, Cole," she greeted warmly.

She wore her usual flannel and jeans, but this pair had rips in the knees and a fraying hole on one of her thighs. He could barely keep his thoughts tame.

"Morning," he managed to squeeze out.

"Did you sleep well?"

"I slept well enough, thank you."

"Liar. I thought you hated lies and head games. Don't tell me you're going to start breaking your own rules now."

Cole clenched his jaw. He wasn't prepared for her smugness so early in the morning. "Fine. I hardly slept a wink. Happy?"

"Very much."

Her smile practically knocked him over. "What about

you?"

She stretched exaggeratedly. "Like a baby." Before he could say more, she shushed him. "Jonas is coming."

"Morning, Cole," Jonas greeted as he handed him a cup of coffee from a takeout joint and a cherry Danish wrapped in wax paper. "Crys and I woke up early and grabbed some breakfast for the group."

Cole looked at his pastry. Finger holes filled the top, and a huge bite was missing from the side. "Looks like someone molested it."

Jonas blamed Crys for the damage, and she giggled, offering no apology.

The thought of her fingering his food should've disgusted him. But he took a huge bite and made sure she watched him lick the cherry sauce from his lips.

"So, did you kids have fun after we went to bed?" Jonas asked, grinning.

"I don't know, did we? You were the one eavesdropping."

Jonas's smile fell. "In my defense, Cole, I was only there to pull Ava away."

Regardless of who listened in on the start of their conversation, Cole made sure to play up his part. "Ava can hope all she wants. Crys and I are never going to date."

To his surprise, Crys interjected with her own

perspective on the relationship. "Yeah, Cole and I talked about it last night, pretty extensively actually. And we both feel that it wouldn't be a good idea, especially since I'm Ava's friend, and...the fact that I'm not ready to date right now. My priority is finding a place to live—which Cole has volunteered to help me with. Tonight. Isn't that right?"

Cole looked at her, his mouth full. "I did?"

A lot was said last night, but he didn't recall that. As he looked at her in confusion, she widened her eyes and nonchalantly gestured toward Jonas.

"Yeah, remember you said you'd be happy to drive me around Meeteetse after work?"

He swallowed what was left in his mouth and realized what Crys was trying to accomplish with the fabricated story. "Right. I did say that."

Jonas shot him an odd look, upon which Cole felt he needed to explain his forgetfulness.

"It was late, and I think I had a few too many beers. But yes, I'm going to drive Crys around town...and help her find a place. To live. In Meeteetse. Just as friends."

Crys patted his back, shutting him up. "I think he's got it, Cole."

Jonas regarded their strange behavior, then said, "Well, if you two want to get out of here before nightfall, we need to get a move on. We've got about ten riders coming at eight o'clock. Forty, I think, for the whole day. So, Crys, if you'd like to start watering and graining the horses that are in this barn, that'd be great. Afterward, you can move to those in the other barn, do the same. Once that's finished, ten of them will need to be saddled and ready to go at the hitching posts outside. Our college girls should be showing up soon, and they'll be mucking and helping you get ready for the first trail ride tour." He checked the time on his cell and shoved it back in his pocket. "Ava should be out within the hour. Right now, she and Rhonda are printing all the liability release and ride consent forms for the day. Any questions?"

"When I'm finished taking care of the horses, am I on trail ride duty with Ava or working cattle with you guys?"

Cole took another bite of his Danish so he didn't have to talk and entrusted Jonas to answer this one. If left up to him, he'd demand she work as far away from him as possible.

"I'd say since it's your first day, let's keep you with Ava. You won't be able to lead the tours since you're not familiar with the trails yet, but you can hold the rear. Make sure there are no stragglers. We can't lose the city folk out here in the wild."

"What about a rifle?" Crys asked, wagging her brow. "I get one of those, don't I?"

"Not until we see how you shoot." Jonas nudged Cole. "Maybe you can convince this guy to target practice with you."

"Seriously?" Crys said, plopping her hands on her hips. "I have to earn a rifle?"

"Around here, you do." Jonas nodded. "There are bigger things in these mountains than what you're used to."

Cole grinned behind his coffee cup. "Unless you brought some ferocious armadillos with you, that shotgun ain't going to do shit for the bears and mountain lions up here. And shooting a rifle is a lot different, sweetheart."

He saw her posture stiffen and wondered what would come out of her mouth next.

"Fine. I'm not afraid to prove I can shoot."

"It's not me you have to impress. It's Cole, here. He's the gun expert."

Crys swiveled her gaze to Cole and waggled her brows. "Then you better bring your A game, cowboy."

Jonas and Cole stood in silence as she marched down the aisle of the barn. It didn't take a genius to see the conceit in her stride. Crys was back to being full of piss and vinegar, and as much as Cole preferred her sweeter side, he knew it would be near impossible to coax it back.

"My A game?" Cole asked. "I always bring my A game."

"Yeah, well I think she's bringing animosity. Good luck with that."

Cole thought about the kiss he and Crys shared last night. There was definitely no animosity then.

Yeah, Jonas might have been fooled, but Cole knew the signs.

Crys was as wild about him as he was about her.

Chapter Twelve

Crys put in a long ten-hour day and loved every minute of it. She was in her glory, surrounded by horses, hay, manure, and leather, in a way that didn't involve strenuous training or intense competition. The sweat she worked up today gave her a newfound respect for the other side of the equine business.

In Houston, it was always about the training, constantly racing to beat your best time. But here, amid the vast blue sky and the towering regal mountains, it was more about the simpler things in life. Caring for the horses. Sharing a smile. Encouraging the apprehensive, first-time folks there was nothing to fear from a twelve-hundred-pound animal as long as they respected it. And making sure that every customer enjoyed their time spent on dead-broke horses with lazy gaits. If she had any doubts about making a life for herself in Meeteetse, they were long gone.

Everything about this place appealed to her. From the vibrant and helpful females on staff, to the eager, novice horseback riders who listened to her every instruction, Crys found an unexpected sense of belonging that she never had in all her years of winning races.

Out of everything she did that day, riding Jericho through the wilderness of Wyoming's breathtaking landscape was her favorite. It was the first time she'd ridden solely for pleasure. She even believed Jericho preferred trail riding to barrel racing. Instead of ears alert and muscles tense, his head hung low, perfectly content to follow the horse in front of him.

At the end of the last trail ride for the day, Crys knew she'd found the perfect job. Now all she needed to do was find the perfect farm for her and Jericho. Coming down the ridge behind twelve riders in a single file, she felt excited about taking that very next step with Cole as her chauffer. She'd kind of blindsided him with those plans this morning, and wondered if he was still up for it.

Madeline and Jolee stood at the barn, waiting to help tie up the returning horses. Hayden and Addison soon joined them and assisted the riders in dismounting. After Crys tied Jericho to the post, she lent a hand to a five-year-old boy struggling to get out of his saddle. He'd been one of the few who were afraid to ride, especially upon meeting his steed, and she had to use a little coaxing to get him close enough to pet the animal. Now, he wanted to take the horse home.

"Please, Mommy," the little boy begged as he pressed himself against the gelding's chest. "I want a horse."

"Honey," the mother said, unbuckling her son's helmet. "We don't have room for a horse."

"He can stay in *my* room."

Crys and the mother laughed at the child's literal perception. "Hey there, partner," Crys said as she squatted on bended knee. "I can see you're pretty fond of this horse. But he's also very fond of *his* home. I don't think he'd want to leave his wide-open pasture for a little bedroom. You know what I mean?"

The boy hung his head and frowned. "Yeah…"

"Horses need room to run and play, just like you. But I'll tell you what. If your family ever comes back here to ride, I'll make sure you get this horse again. Okay?" Crys held out her upturned palm and waited. After some thought, the boy slapped her hand as hard as he could. "Wow, you're strong. Cowboy strong," Crys emphasized.

The boy beamed and smiled at his mom. She took his hand and thanked Crys for all she did. Crys waved good-bye and watched the boy strut back to their shiny SUV in his dusty little boots.

"You certainly made him happy," Ava remarked as she led two horses into the barn to untack.

"Yeah, well, he's five. It doesn't take much to please that age group."

Ava glanced back at the mother who struggled to get her rambunctious son buckled in the backseat. "I think Mom might beg to differ on that one."

Crys laughed and thanked her lucky stars she only had a dozen horses to care for. She'd take a handful of wild horses over a one unruly child. As she led Jericho and the boy's horse into the barn, she found it strange to even contemplate having children. Her own parents weren't exactly the best role models, and being the baby of the family, she didn't know much about raising kids in general. The only thing she knew how to do well was train, travel, and compete against other adult riders. Her only experience with kids was signing their autographs, encouraging them to work hard, and shoot for their dreams.

"You ever think about kids, Crys?" Ava asked, lugging two saddles to the tack room.

"Honestly? Not until just now." Crys unfastened Jericho's girth strap and wondered why she admitted something like that to Ava. "What about you?"

She heard Ava laugh. "Kids? No. I'm too old."

"Is Jonas okay with not having kids? I mean, since you guys are getting married now."

Crys watched Ava's reaction as she came out of the

tack room and removed the headstalls from her horses. A frown creased her lips. "I guess he's okay with that. We never really talked about it."

"Talked about what?"

Jonas's deep voice erupted from behind them as he entered the barn. Cole, Rod, and Brody were with him, their gazes fixed on Crys.

She hid her excitement at seeing Cole again. She could feel his weighty stare on her body as if he were undressing her right there in front of everyone. His face remained emotionless, but the way his full lips thinned to a straight line proved he had a hard time resisting his baser urges.

Rod strutted in with a cocky smile, one that matched his swaggering stride. He was built much like his brother, tall and broad. He even equaled Brody in the good looks department. But while Rod possessed the carefree arrogance of a bona fide playboy, Brody entertained a more serious look, similar to Cole's brooding nature. Though reserved at the moment, she imagined Brody was a powerhouse of a man who could inflict serious damage when provoked.

"Kids," Ava stated, looking mildly nervous with the whole subject. "We never really talked about having kids."

Jonas drew back. "You want another one? At your age?"

Ava pinned him with a glare. "At my age...not really. Do you?"

Jonas took Ava in his arms, kissed her on the mouth, and flashed a dimply smile to smooth over his misspoken words. "I want whatever makes you happy, Trick."

In seeing Ava go from offended to flattered in two seconds flat, Crys thought it was downright ridiculous how easily Jonas charmed her.

"My happiness is knowing I'm giving you everything you've ever hoped for, Jonas." Ava fiddled with the hood strings on Jonas's coat. "And if that's kids—"

"I have a kid. Your kid. I'm just thrilled he's potty trained."

Ava slugged his arm. "I'm serious, Jonas."

"So am I. I'm proud to call Sawyer my son."

"Aw...isn't that sweet?" Rod chimed in, laying it on thick. "Don't you just love happy endings?"

"So, you must be Rod," Crys said matter-of-factly.

His face lit up, and he sidled up next to Jericho with an outstretched hand. "Why yes, I'm Rod Galven. And you are?"

Jonas swiveled in Ava's arms, realizing he'd forgotten some much needed introductions. "Sorry, guys. Rod, Brody, this is Crystal Willingham, Ava's friend from the rodeo circuit. She's come all the way from Houston, looking for a place to hang her hat."

Rod clasped her hand in his. "In Meeteetse, I can only hope?"

Crys regarded the length of time he continued to hold her hand. She hated to give this man the impression that he'd have anything to do with whether or not she chose this place over Big Horn. If any man was doing that, it was Cole. "I'm still undecided."

"Wait a minute," Rod broke in, saying her full name again. "Are you *the* Crystal Willingham, the championship barrel racer? The one who went undefeated three years in a row?"

Crys sustained many records in her time, some that still stood to this day, but she never was the kind to brag. "I reckon that'd be me, at one time or another."

"Well, flip my switch and call me shocked! I can't believe I'm standing in the presence of a celebrity."

Crys glanced at Cole and noticed the intensity of his stare. He looked as if he were two seconds away from grabbing Rod by his coat and tossing him out of the barn. She pulled her hand from Rod's as politely as she could. "I wouldn't go that far."

"Darlin', there's tons of women who'd give anything to stand in your shoes." Rod leaned in closer. "So, tell me. What's your total career earnings now?"

"Rod," Jonas warned.

"Well, it's not like I can't google it and find out. It's public knowledge as far as the NFR is concerned."

Rod was correct in that her career earnings were posted on many public forums and sites, including her current year's win and how many times she qualified in the National Finals Rodeo. But she still felt uneasy admitting anything about her cash yield landing in the neighborhood of seven hundred thousand.

"Then I guess you're going to have to google it, Rod," Crys replied snarkily. "Unless you're the IRS, I don't think it's necessary that you know what I've earned in my career."

"Oh, c'mon, admit it. It's got to be over a half million by now, right?"

Crys sighed, knowing Rod wasn't going to let up until she gave him something. "Let's just say you're close."

"I knew it! And, I take it that sweet truck and trailer outside are yours too?"

"Yes, they are."

With Rod bringing up the subject of her vehicle, she recalled Jonas mentioning Brody and his skills for mechanic work. She'd been so preoccupied with Cole that she almost forgot about her truck troubles. She stepped around Rod and extended her hand to his brother.

"Speaking of my truck...Brody, I hear you might be

able to take a look at it?"

Brody shook her hand, but unlike his brother, he clasped her hand long enough to pump it once and let go. He remained reserved and a complete gentleman.

"Yes, ma'am. Jonas had me take a look at it this morning while you were out on the trail, and it's nothing serious. It seems that something punctured your radiator and caused a leak. A rock or a bird, I'm guessing. Whatever it was did damage to your grill too. I put a call in to the dealership in Cody and ordered the parts. I'll head up that way first thing in the morning, but unfortunately, it'll take all of tomorrow to finish. I was hoping to have it up and running sooner since Jonas said you were looking to scout the area for a place to live. But tomorrow is the best I can do, ma'am."

Crys sighed with relief. "That's okay. I just appreciate you fixing it for me, Brody."

"It's not a problem."

"I wouldn't mind giving you a lift around town," Rod offered as he touched her shoulder. "In fact, I'd be honored to show you all that Meeteetse has to offer. Maybe even grab some dinner afterward?"

Crys glanced at Cole and watched the muscle in his jaw flex.

"I appreciate that, Rod, but it seems Cole beat you to

it."

Rod didn't hide his surprise. "You two have already met?"

Cole locked gazes with Crys. Without saying a word, he conveyed his anguish over exposing the dirty details of how they met to someone like Rod. She could almost hear him saying, *For the love of God, keep your mouth shut, Crys.*

Truth be told, she didn't want Rod to know she'd pulled a gun on Cole any more than Cole did. In the few moments she'd spent with Rod, she realized he was a man who had a knack for prying into people's business whether they liked it or not. She had enough of that from her father and three brothers back home.

If anything, Rod made her appreciate Cole's quiet demeanor that much more. There was nothing wrong with the handsome Galven brother. She could even imagine that most women would die for a chance to have Rod's undivided attention. But that kind of smothering behavior did nothing for her.

She preferred a man who retained a degree of intrigue by keeping some things a mystery. A man who was content with not having to know everything under the sun and leaving some stuff to the imagination.

A man like Cole.

"Yes, we already met this weekend when I drove in

from Houston. Out of the kindness of her heart, Ava made dinner for the four of us last night, and Cole offered once he knew I didn't have a working truck."

Rod cracked a smile. "Then you've spent enough time with him to know he's one cranky ol' cowboy. You sure you still wanna go with him?"

Cole's brown eyes turned black. "By all means, Crys, don't let me stop you."

Crys would've bet her entire career earnings Cole didn't mean a word he said. Taking into account the scorching kiss they shared last night, she knew he wasn't ready to give up his chance to be with her for anybody—especially Rod.

She pulled her gaze from Cole and directed her next words to Rod. "As much as I'd like that, I'd hate to be rude to the cranky cowboy. Maybe another time."

She imagined Rod wasn't used to being turned down and could see him trying to come to terms with it in his head. "Sure. Another time, then."

Crys could feel every weighty stare from those in the barn who were oblivious to her and Cole's secret pact. Even Ava, who'd eavesdropped on them last night, appeared to wonder about what had gone on between them after Cole had admitted his feelings. It seemed everyone believed that she and Cole didn't particularly get along, and she was only going out of politeness. When in reality, she couldn't wait to get her hands on him.

"Rod, Brody. It was nice to meet you both. Ava, if you don't mind, I'm going to finish with the horses and scoot on out of here while Cole and I still have some daylight left."

"Does that mean you're really thinking of staying in Meeteetse?"

Ava's surprise was no doubt compounded by the fact that she'd been worrying over the issues between Crys and Cole for some time, and that they might affect Crys's decision on choosing Meeteetse for a home. Crys answered in a way that would ease her friend's mind.

"It means I love working here. And despite one such cranky cowboy who'd rather see me live elsewhere, I'm sticking to my guns and not letting any man influence my decisions." She pretended to glower at Cole, selling her statement. "No pun intended."

Chapter Thirteen

"Rod's right, Cole. You are cranky."

It was the first thing Crys had said to him since they climbed in his truck and drove a few miles in total silence. He could see from his peripheral vision that she'd put her pen down and closed the realty magazine she'd been marking in since they left the McKinley ranch. He kept his eyes ahead as he drove down the windy backroad toward his house. "What makes you say that?"

"Because you haven't said two words since we left. Obviously, you're mad about something."

For whatever reason, he suddenly felt the need to look at her. He regarded the way her brows lifted a little higher on her forehead. The way her bottom lip stuck out just a bit farther than her top. The way her blonde hair, braided loosely down the side of her neck, hung like a gorgeous golden rope.

He wanted to tell her how beautiful she was. And how bad he itched to kiss her lips every time he looked at her—

every time he took a breath. But no matter how much he wanted to say those things to her, he wouldn't. It was way too soon. And running her off before he even had a chance to kiss her again was a risk he wasn't willing to take.

He didn't know much about the barrel racer who'd abandoned her career just when she'd made it to the top, except for two things. One—that she was done with sitting in the passenger seat, and two—that she wasn't afraid to take chances. While the latter might work in his favor for stealing another kiss, the other kept him from doing something more in haste.

He had thought that with insisting they sleep on it, the time away from her would give him twenty-four hours to come to his senses. But now that a full day had come and gone, he was no wiser than before he kissed her.

"I'm not mad. I'm just wondering if I can do this."

"This…meaning driving me around, looking for property?"

"Yep." He didn't have to look at Crys to know he left her confused.

"I don't understand. What's so hard about looking at farms and houses in a town you're familiar with?"

Cole bit down, holding back the words that threatened to slip from his mouth. "Everything. Just trust me on this."

He heard her toss the pen and real estate book on the

seat between them.

"You're going to have to be more specific, Cole. If it's because you can't deal with the fact that I'm considering living in Meeteetse, then—"

"It's not that. You can live wherever you damn well please."

"Then what is it?"

Cole made the turn into his drive a little too fast, and the momentum threw her against the passenger-side door with Sammy scrambling for traction on the leather seat.

Crys began chewing him a new one for his reckless driving, but he ignored every bit of it. After sliding the truck to a halt and throwing the shifter into Park, he turned to face her and slammed his fist on the dash to shut her up.

"I can't drive all around town, with you sitting next to me—well within my reach—and keep my hands off you. I can't. I barely made it the few miles to my house. All I can think about since kissing you last night is how badly I want to do it again. That's what I want, and I can't think of anything else. So, your little plan to hang out and mosey around town like we're just friends might sound great to you, but for me, it's torture."

In the silence that followed, Cole realized he'd said too much and too harshly. The look of shock on her face nearly killed him.

He sighed and slumped behind the steering wheel, tossing his cowboy hat on the dash. He let his head thud against the door window and dragged his hands down his face, regretting everything he'd done up to this point.

"Maybe you should've gone with Rod. You would've at least gotten a free dinner out of him."

Sammy placed his front paws on the dash, sniffed his hat, and wagged his tail. Glad to be home, he barked and gave Cole a look of expectancy.

Cole sighed and opened the truck door. Sammy jumped out and immediately scoured the yard for new scents. By the time he zigzagged his way to the barn, Crys had scooted across the seat toward Cole. She placed both hands on his thighs and leaned in, capturing his full attention.

He hadn't prepared for this. She smelled of coconut shampoo and mixed with the scent of whatever perfume she'd sprayed on her neck that morning. It was an intoxicating aroma. He wanted that fragrance all over his clothes. All over his bedsheets.

"I don't want Rod," she whispered. "I don't want dinner."

Cole swallowed, waiting patiently for her to admit what she *did* want. When it was clear she wasn't going to specify her desires, he asked her point-blank. "What *do* you want,

Crys?"

She brought her face closer. He saw her glance down at his lips before she took his in a slow, sensual kiss that rocked his world.

He yearned to reach for her, but instead, he willed his hands to stay where they were, clenched in tight fists at his side. Even when she whimpered in his mouth and climbed in his lap, he remained frozen.

Crys pulled out of the kiss and stared at him as if trying to fathom why he hadn't moved a muscle. "You're going to make me say it, aren't you?"

"You have to."

Crys smiled and ran both her hands up his neck and into his hair. Her fingertips dug into his scalp, massaging the tension he'd accumulated in the past three days while she breathed in his ear and bit his lobe. Chills trickled through his spine as hot blood coursed through his veins. His self-control thinned to almost nonexistent.

"I'm going out of my mind here, Crys. Say what you want."

Her hands paused, and she sat up. "Isn't it obvious by now?"

Cole closed his eyes and drew in a long breath. "Nothing is obvious to me. Between the thousandth time I've kissed you in my head and the things you're doing to me now, everything is blurred."

Crys smiled as if humored by the way his last word came out in a growl. He didn't think any of it was funny.

He felt her hands slide to the nape of his neck. She held firm, and she repositioned her body higher up on his hips.

Her smile faded as she straddled him. "You know what I want, Cole? I want you to stop pretending you can't make decisions for yourself. I already made mine this morning after sleeping on it. It's the reason I'm sitting in your truck right now. I could've gone with Rod, and by this time I probably could've actually set foot on a few farms I circled in the realty magazine on the way here. But I don't give a crap about that. All I want is you. But you have to figure out what *you* want. You're the one with all the rules, all the conditions you feel necessary to put on our relationship in order to make yourself feel better about being with me. You want honesty? I'll give you the God's honest truth every single time you ask. But until you come clean with yourself, none of this will work."

Chapter Fourteen

Crys never expected to say the things she said. When he took hold of her arms and gently eased her off his lap, she was even more surprised that he finally touched her.

"You're right," he uttered as he faced the steering wheel. He took hold of it with both hands and shook his head. "This isn't going to work."

She watched him close his eyes and take a deep breath. She had no idea what he was doing, what he was thinking as he sat there in some weird meditative state. After a few seconds of awkward silence, his eyes flashed open and he picked his hat up off the dash. Placing it back on his head, he opened the truck door and hopped out.

Crys sat stunned, unable to feel her legs as he slammed the door shut and walked toward his house. A pang of disappointment pierced her chest, followed by anger. She saw red, a rush of needles prickling in her veins as she realized he'd deserted her. Shunned by the one man she wanted more than anything since she arrived in Meeteetse.

Cole stopped short of his porch and turned his head. He peered at her from under the brim of his hat and planted his hands on his hips. His handsome, chiseled face, though she wanted to punch it, expressed a look of smug satisfaction.

She wanted to yell at him. To flip him off and drive herself back to the McKinley ranch using his own truck so he could feel what it felt like to be left in the dust. But she couldn't do anything but seethe inside his cab.

"Are you coming?" Cole finally spoke. "Or do I have to drag you out of the truck?"

Crys's mouth fell open, but she closed it as soon as his words registered.

A slow, joyful smile split her lips, and her heart kicked into a happy buck. She wasted no time scrambling out of the vehicle, almost tripping on her feet as she ran to him. The delight in Cole's eyes tickled her insides, and she couldn't get to him fast enough.

Crys leapt into his arms, and he caught her, kissing her as he held her tight against him. She still wanted to punch him in the face for making her think he was disinterested. But the feel of his tender lips and strong embrace softened the blow to her pride.

Tangled up in each other's arms, they stumbled up the porch steps and staggered through the front door. Upon bouncing off the inside stair railing, Crys pulled out of his kiss and looked around.

They stood in a one-room log home with a bedroom loft, and an impressive floor-to-ceiling rock fireplace. On it hung a giant bull elk mount, a big-screen TV, and a manly, single-beam pine mantel, the basic components of a bachelor's lodge.

"Did you build this yourself?"

"Most of it."

His kitchen table was small, with only two chairs perfectly pushed in. His coffee table, on the other hand, was a large sheet of glass dadoed into a wooden barrel cut lengthwise in half. She took a guess that he hardly ever used the one in the kitchen given the mess of empty plates, beer bottles, and chip bags covering the other. Like his coffee table, blankets and pillows spilled over the side of his leather couch, proving he spent more time eating and sleeping in his living room than he did in the designated areas of his home.

"You really are a bachelor through and through, aren't ya?"

Cole curled his fingers between his lips and blew out a sharp whistle. Within seconds, Sammy ran inside the front door to a bowl beside the coffee table. He lapped his water like he hadn't drank in days, spilling droplets all over the hardwood floor.

"Including your dog, I see."

"It's the only life we know."

Cole shut the door and removed his cowboy hat and coat. He hung them up on the wall behind him, then helped her out of hers. She noticed he didn't have a second hook for her apparel. "You don't entertain much either."

"Never saw the point in it."

Spoken like a true hermit.

If anything, Cole's stance on limited visitors made her feel better about the kind of bachelor he was. He lived a solitary life with only his dog as a companion, and he seemed perfectly content. With everything she saw in his meager home, it was obvious he hadn't built it to accommodate a woman in his future. In fact, she wondered if she were the first female to even grace his door.

Cole hung her things over the banister and scooped her up in his arms. "You done looking around?"

She smiled and wrapped her arms around his neck. "I thought you'd never ask."

Cole's deep laughter sent shock waves through her body as he carried her up the stairs. When he crested the top, he tossed her on the bed like a sack of grain.

A sound of surprise slipped from her mouth as she bounced on his neatly made king-sized bed. Collecting her bearings, she regarded the thick western-style comforter with a design of horseshoes and rope beneath her palms. Much to her liking, it was an extremely comfortable mattress. She'd spent too many nights in a cramped trailer, and she welcomed the luxury of his large, cozy bed. She wondered why he didn't.

"How come you don't sleep here?"

Cole had already begun unbuttoning his shirt. "I work long hours. Hauling hay, fixing fence, roping and driving cattle, you name it. I'm either on my feet or riding a saddle all day. When I come home, I couldn't care less where I crash. As long as I'm horizontal."

Cole popped the last few buttons on his shirt, and Crys sat mesmerized, anxious to see the hard, muscled body she knew he had to have. Her mouth practically watered over the thought of running her hands along every toned inch of him.

"And before I get horizontal with you," he added, unbuckling his belt, "I need a shower. I smell like cow shit."

Crys gawked at the definitive V-shaped platform of muscles that ran along his hips and disappeared into his pants. "I hadn't noticed."

Cole smiled, chucking his shirt and belt. "Feel free to make yourself comfortable. I'll only be a few minutes."

He stepped into the bathroom across from the bed and shut the door behind him, leaving Crys with a mental picture of him stripping out of the rest of his clothes. As she heard the shower come on, she envisioned him standing under a gentle spray of water, naked and soapy.

She'd never longed for a man as bad as she did him and wondered how she was going get through this night without falling for him.

This was just supposed to be a fling, a little fun to have while she looked for a permanent residence in Meeteetse. She wasn't supposed to get all hung up on a guy before she even found a place to live.

But she was.

And there was no use fighting it.

Resisting Cole would take more willpower than she possessed, and she'd already begun to feel it cave after that first, phenomenal kiss. She could only imagine how hard she'd fall once he laid his big, strapping body on top of her.

Just thinking about it made her jittery and restless. Even when she'd been up against the steepest competition in the NFR, she never suffered this kind of nervousness.

Unable to sit still, she slid off the bed and paced the loft. Upon hearing her stir, Sammy came running up the stairs. She knelt on bended knee and petted him as he wagged his tail with glee.

"Keeping me company, huh?"

Sammy offered his paw and a serious case of puppy dog eyes. She shook his paw and smiled. "Well, aren't you the sweetest?"

In submission, Sammy rolled over on his back and bared his belly. Crys rubbed his stomach in return. "You got it made, you know that? You get to hang out with him every single day, without anyone questioning why. I wish I had that luxury."

Sammy whined, and she drifted into her own thoughts. She should have been thrilled that she'd gotten Cole to break his rule for her, especially after hearing how badly he wanted her.

Like no man has ever wanted you.

Those words alone were awe-inspiring, especially since he wasn't the type to even admit such a thing. But the truth was that while they agreed to see each other in secret, she worried about the amount of trouble they'd have to go through to keep it that way. What's more, she wondered when all was said and done if her heart would make it out in one piece.

As she scratched Sammy's roan fur, she noticed a jagged scar running the length of his hind leg. She ran her finger along it, surprised that he allowed her to inspect it so closely. "What happened here, boy?"

"A grizzly got a hold of him."

Crys gasped at the sound of Cole's voice behind her. When she spun to face him, the sight of him standing in nothing but a towel bowled her over like the head butt of a charging bull.

Chapter Fifteen

The images of what Crys thought Cole's ripped body might look like didn't hold a candle to the real deal. He was far more magnificent than she could've ever imagined, and she couldn't stop staring. It was the first time she saw him without clothes, and, like magic, the subject of Sammy's heinous scar vanished from her train of thought. All that registered was him.

She stood and felt her legs wobble beneath her. "Wow, that was fast. I didn't expect you to finish so soon."

"Some things I do in haste."

Cole's eyes darkened as he came near, alluding to the fact that he didn't intend to rush through anything beyond his shower. He smelled of soap—something very masculine—and she yearned to bury her face in his neck. To breathe him in like pure oxygen.

Her fingers trembled as she dared to touch his bare chest. "Can I..." Her words fell short as she reached out. She could barely do what her mind so desperately wanted without his permission.

"Touch me?" His voice was husky and wickedly sexy. "I wish you would."

She closed her eyes and laid her hand on his chest. His skin was still damp, yet warm beneath her fingers. It was the most erotic thing to feel such hard muscle beneath such smooth skin.

"Were you," he started to ask, "talking to my dog?"

Her eyes shot open. Though she'd heard Cole converse with his dog many times, it sounded absurd to know she had. "Yeah?"

Cole grinned. "I hope you know that conversation's over." He glanced down at Sammy and gestured with his head. "Beat it, boy."

"Aww..." Crys whined, watching the dog trot down the stairs. "Let him stay."

"I don't think so. I do better without an audience." Cole grabbed her by the hips and pulled her against him. His half-spoken promise held so much heat, she felt the burn as if he'd actually struck a match.

"You have no idea how bad I want you, do you?" he asked.

She stared into his big brown eyes, relishing the power and strength of his body hovering over hers. She wrapped her arms around his neck and tried to corral enough brain cells to answer him.

"I think I do."

He smiled again, but this time it lit up his whole face. The sparkle in his chestnut eyes turned the rascally rogue into the boy next door, with a mouth so perfect and so kissable. Unable to resist, she pulled him down and kissed his lips.

She wondered if this hard-nosed cowboy would ever admit to falling in love. He was brave enough to confess his attraction to her, despite the fact that he fought it tooth and nail, but would he be man enough to acknowledge something deeper?

Crazier things had happened.

Out of everything she'd come to know about the sexy giant, his kiss was the best. Because through his tenderness, she could feel the truth of his words come to life.

"I want you, Crys Willingham, like no man has ever wanted you."

She opened her eyes as their slow, sensual kiss ended and found him staring at her. She felt her cheeks blush.

"I've never seen anyone as beautiful as you."

She quivered as she felt his touch on her back beneath her shirt. She wished he'd just take it off.

"Cole, you don't have to do this. It's me remember? I don't need frills or flattery. You know what I need."

"I wasn't saying that because you needed to hear it. I said it because it's true." Cole swept her up and laid her on the bed. With his hands braced on either side of her, he hovered. "Now shut your mouth and let me do what I do best."

****

Crys felt Cole's breath, hot and forceful on her neck, as his massive body lay upon hers. Wrapping her arms around him, she pulled him closer and let out a breathless 'wow'.

"Wow means good?"

His deep voice rumbled against her throat. She couldn't tamp down her smile as she twirled her fingers in his damp hair. "Wow means better than good."

"Well, I did bring my A game."

"Oh, whatever. I'm sure you bring your A game with all the ladies."

With one laborious push, Cole rolled off her and sank into the mattress on his back. He stared at the ceiling for the span of a few breaths and said, "True... but this might be the first time I cared enough to make sure I brought it."

Crys sat up on her elbow, trying to read the blank expression on his face. "What do you mean, cared enough?

Cared about what?"

"About everything." He looked at her now, a trace of vulnerability flashing in his eyes. He lifted his hand and caressed her cheek. "I don't know what it is about you, Angel, but you make me feel things I've never felt before. And I don't know how to deal with it. From the second I laid eyes on you, I wanted you. What's crazy is, now that I've had you, I still want more. I thought if I could just have you for one night, I'd get you out of my system."

"How's that going for you?"

Crys noticed the muscle in his jaw flex before he let out a laugh.

"Not so good actually."

For a few seconds, she smiled at his jest, then sat up on one elbow. "All jokes aside, are you okay with that?"

Cole had always enjoyed women, but never to the same caliber as he enjoyed Crys. There was something different about her that excited him physically, something deeper than just the carnal act of sex.

When he gazed into her eyes, he witnessed his own reflection. For each moment he glimpsed at himself, weak and vulnerable, he stared back at a man, confident and virile.

When he heard his name on Crys's lips, he somehow

knew he no longer wanted to hear another woman's voice in his ears. Only hers could bring him this much life-altering awareness.

"Yeah, I think I am okay with that,' he finally admitted.

He pulled her body close, cherishing the feel of her tiny frame butted against his. The softness of her skin and the bow of her curves felt so right in his arms that he didn't even mind when she snuggled closer.

Better yet, she didn't ask him to talk about his feelings. Like him, she was perfectly content to lie with him in silence and let the blissful moment simmer around them.

Though nothing was said for the next half hour, he still couldn't keep his hands off her. Whether he stroked her hair, kissed her neck, or absently dragged his fingertips along her arm, he'd done all these things as easily as if he'd done them countless times before.

Touching Crys seemed natural, and for once in his life, he found comfort in picturing her presence on a daily basis. He could see her curling up with him on the couch to watch a movie after a long day's work, or waking up to the smell of her cooking breakfast in the kitchen. He could even get used to having long-winded conversations with her, and it didn't matter if she were the one doing all the talking. Nothing he could imagine was a reason to kick her to the curb like he'd done with every other girl he'd met before her.

"You know," she whispered, breaking the silence of the room. "You don't have to spoon me."

Cole stilled. "Do you not like it?"

As he moved to release his embrace, she pulled his arm back down around her. "No, I love it."

"So, what's the problem?"

She hesitated, drumming her fingers on his forearm. "I can tell you're not the kind of guy who normally does this sort of thing."

"You're right. I'm not."

She swiveled her body to face him. "I want you to know you don't have to do it on my account."

Cole smiled and brushed back a strand of her hair. "Trust me. I'm doing it purely for selfish reasons."

"Is everything you've done tonight for selfish reasons?"

He grinned from ear to ear. "I'm not sure how to answer that."

"You can start by telling the truth."

"Okay, fine. I admit in the beginning, it was all for greed. All for me."

"And now?" she joked playfully.

"It's all for you, baby."

She shoved his laughing face away and giggled with

him. "And don't you forget it, cowboy."

He couldn't forget anything they'd done that night if he tried. Every sweet memory was branded in his brain.

Out of all of it, her laughter was the best. The easy merriment they shared reminded him of Jonas and Ava, and it left him with an understanding for why his best friend had settled down with a woman who'd brought him so much joy.

As Crys relaxed in his arms, and nuzzled in tight, a bit of disappointment came over him.

"What's wrong?" she asked, drawing circles on his chest.

"It's getting late. If I don't have you back soon, Ava's going to think something's up."

"So, you still want to keep this between us?"

Cole ignored the voice in his head. "I reckon it's best. For everyone. For now."

He regarded her closely, looking for a reason to change his mind. But she offered nothing by way of expression. A poker face was all he got.

"Look, Crys, just so you know, I've never lied to my friends, and I'm not going to start now. But as long as they don't ask, I'm not going to tell."

"I couldn't agree more." She rolled out of his arms and leapt from the bed.

As he lay there, watching her get dressed, he realized it wasn't so easy. Every fiber of his being longed to pull her back into bed and to forget about keeping their relationship a secret.

Forget my rule, and stay with me tonight.

The words rested on the tip of his tongue, but he couldn't spit them out. She'd already slipped on her jeans and was buttoning the last few buttons on her shirt. For someone who dressed that fast, she didn't look like a woman who wanted to stay.

So, he tamped down his emotions and grabbed some clothes from his dresser drawer. "You hungry?"

Crys patted her empty stomach. "Starving."

He walked toward her as he buttoned his fly. "You should've said something." He wrapped his arms around her, treasuring his last opportunity to feel her body against his. "I've got peanut butter and jelly."

"PB&J sounds great. Come on, I'll help you make them." She slipped from his arms and swatted his butt before jogging down the stairs.

Sammy met her at the bottom, barking and wagging his tail. As Cole watched his dog follow on her heels from the loft above, he concluded that he couldn't blame Sammy for taking to her so fondly.

Cole might have awoken this morning with the

determination to resist Crys, but now, rule or no rule, he was ready to ride this fling for as long as she'd let him.

Chapter Sixteen

Cole woke early, ready to start the day, regardless that he barely slept.

Again.

After he'd dropped Crys off at the McKinley's', he couldn't wind down, and lying in a bed full of recent passionate memories hadn't helped matters.

He'd entertained the idea of hitting the couch, but he couldn't peel himself away from the pillows and sheets that smelled like her. If anything, the time he spent awake gave him the opportunity to figure out a way to see more of Crys without anyone knowing. It was going to suck driving back and forth from his place to her trailer every night, and he needed a good excuse for why her trailer needed to be at his ranch versus Jonas's.

Six hours later and running on fumes, Cole came up empty.

Maybe Crys would have an idea.

Anxious to see her again, he dressed, brewed a pot of

coffee, brushed his teeth, and left the house in fifteen minutes flat. He tore down the road with the thought of Crys's kiss on his mind, hoping he could snag one before anyone arrived for work.

Pulling in quietly, he leapt from his truck with two travel coffee mugs in hand, Sammy on his heels. Noting that not even Jonas had ventured from his house to the barn, he slipped between Crys's truck and trailer and rapped quietly on her door.

The trailer shifted on its jacks, and his heart kicked up in anticipation of seeing her fresh out of bed. When her door opened, he smiled.

Crys was dressed in nothing but an oversized T, her shapely legs pressed close together as if she were cold. Reminiscent of last night, her hair hung past her shoulders in a tangled mess. Her baby blues, once wide and full of hunger, now squinted at him through the bright morning sunlight.

"Good morning," he said, handing her a piping hot cup of coffee.

She leaned against the frame and accepted his gift with a bright smile. "Good morning, Cole." Sammy placed his front paws on the aluminum step of her trailer, wagging his tail in greeting. She reached down and patted his head. "And good morning to you too, Sam."

Cole noticed the sluggish manner in which she moved. "I take it you didn't sleep well either?"

"Hardly a wink." She yawned. "But it was worth it." She looked around him toward the McKinley home. "Jonas isn't stirring?"

"Not *yet*."

It was obvious she knew exactly what he insinuated. With the trailer floor affording her the height of an extra foot, she stood eye to eye with him and leaned out the door to kiss him. Not only did she smell like heaven, but her kisses were heavenly sweet.

Knowing better than to wrap his arms around her— because he wouldn't be able to let go—he forced himself to keep the kiss tame.

"Would you like to come in?" she asked.

He fought the urge to say yes. "No. I mean, yes, I do, but I shouldn't." His struggle produced a smile on her lips so wicked, he wanted to ravish that mouth with an equal kiss or better.

As soon as Cole leaned in, Sammy's ears perked. When his dog bolted, he knew it could only mean one thing: Jonas was coming.

"Hurry, get back inside," he whispered. "And put that coffee in a different mug. Jonas'll recognize mine." In all the excitement, just as he was about to slip away, she slammed the door. Cole stopped dead in his tracks, cringing at the thought of Jonas hearing it.

He glanced at her window and saw Crys peeking through the glass. *Sorry*, she mouthed.

Cole had no idea how he would explain the fact that he was visiting with Crys so early in the morning. His mind was already in a whirlwind.

Before he could sneak away, Jonas turned the corner of Crys's trailer. Cole stood there with a dumbfounded look on his face.

"I take it she hasn't eased up on that animosity?" Jonas asked.

Cole hesitated, then recalled why Jonas had thought that. Turned out Crys slamming her door was the best thing that could've ever happened. "Nope. Still hates me."

Jonas clicked his tongue. "You know, that's a shame. I was really hoping that after you spent some time together driving around Meeteetse, you two could put all this behind you."

Inside, Cole was relieved with how easy Jonas made it to sidestep the truth. "Yeah, no such luck."

Jonas put his hand on Cole's shoulder. "I feel for you buddy, I really do. I know how hard this must be for you to want something you can't have. I assume you're still holding firm to that rule?"

"I am."

"Well, unfortunately, this little situation between you and Crys makes it that much harder for me to ask this favor of you."

Cole liked to think he knew his friend better than anyone. They'd been best friends since kindergarten, through thick and thin, asking their share of favors over the years. But even two and half decades of comradery couldn't help Cole figure out what tied Jonas up in knots.

"You think we can go somewhere else to discuss this in case Ava comes out?"

"Sure. Lead the way."

Together they walked to the barn and stepped inside the tack room. Cole knew it had to be something big when Jonas closed the door behind him. He'd never seen his friend so nervous.

"I need your help, Cole."

"You got it. Whatever you need."

Jonas paced the small room, rubbing the back of his neck. "You know how I asked Ava to marry me a few months ago, right? Well, it would mean everything to me if you'd be my best man."

Cole drew back in confusion. "Of course I'll be your best man. Why would you think otherwise?"

Jonas's feet came to a rest. "It's not that I thought

you'd object to it, it's just that there's more to consider."

"And that is?"

"With Crys in town, looking to stay, Ava wants to ask her to be her maid of honor."

"Seems perfectly logical."

Jonas stared at him wide-eyed. "Realize...you'd have to walk down the aisle with her."

"McKinley, if I can ride in a truck with the woman, I think I can handle walking a few seconds with her down a church aisle."

Jonas went back to pacing. "Good. Okay. So, here's the kicker."

Cole stilled, waiting for the other shoe to fall. What could the man possibly need from him that was too difficult to ask?

"I want to surprise Ava with a wedding. A barn wedding. She's always wanted that, but I can't have it here for obvious reasons. That's where you come in. I want to have it at your place at the end of next month, even though Ava thinks we're going to have it here...next fall."

Cole scratched his head. "You want to have it in my barn. My barn, that's full of equipment, and hay, and God knows what else?"

"I know, I know, it's going to be a huge undertaking to clean it out, but I really want to surprise her. You know how much Ava loves surprises."

If Cole knew anything about Ava, it was her appreciation for the unexpected. And he could easily understand why Jonas wanted to match his shocking proposal with an equally unpredicted wedding. "You know we're right in the middle of fall calving, right?"

"Don't worry. After calving, me and the guys will handle all the chores while you tend to the barn."

"And who's going to decorate it?"

"I was kind of hoping you and Crys could do that."

Cole wanted to smile. He could feel his heart beating harder. Though he didn't know the first thing about decorating, this was the break he'd been looking for. The perfect excuse to spend some serious alone time with Crys without anyone thinking twice. He tried not to look so excited and furrowed his brow on purpose.

"I don't know. That's a lot to ask of me, Jonas."

"I know it is, but I can't think of anything else without Ava getting suspicious. With you stuck at your place, you can just say you're finally getting around to those renovations you've been wanting to tackle. And with Ava knowing how badly Crys wants to find property, she can just say she's house hunting."

Cole was impressed that Jonas had everything worked out for him. "It all sounds good, but when Crys leaves work every night to come help me, what's to keep Ava from coming with her? You know she won't let Crys"—he curled his fingers into quotes—"house hunt alone."

"Already thought of that. I've got Rhonda on board to keep her busy on some nights, and the other evenings I'll step up. Maybe take that damn Pilates class she's been wanting to go to. I just need Rhonda and Crys to somehow figure out what dress Ava wants and what flowers she'd like in the bouquets. You know, that girlie shit."

Cole swiped his hand across his jaw, hiding the grin that threatened to ruin this beautifully laid-out plan. He couldn't have come up with a better one if he tried. What's more, Jonas had given Crys the ideal alibi.

Suppressing his true emotions, he disengaged himself from the matter at hand. "Good luck convincing Crys."

Jonas's head fell back on his shoulders. "Who am I kidding? Crys isn't going to go for this. Not when she finds out I need her to spend more time at your place. But who else is there? Maybe Rhonda can do it... She knows Ava pretty well."

Cole started to feel the rug slip out from beneath him. "Look, I don't know much about weddings, but I'm pretty sure the maid of honor should have a hand in the preparations. And besides, I need someone with a little more muscle and tenacity if you want this barn to be perfect. Even after we clear it out, seating has to be arranged, an altar's got to be built. Does Rhonda even know how to swing a hammer? Or climb a ladder? Maybe she should take care of the dresses. I hear she's pretty talented behind a sewing machine."

"You might be right."

Sell it, Cole. Sell it!

"Crys might be a hard-ass, Jonas, but I think she'll do anything you ask, especially if it's for Ava." He hoped he didn't sound too zealous. "All you can do is ask."

Jonas slapped him on the shoulder, laughing away his worries. "You know what? You're right. She'll do it for Ava. I'll go talk to her. Thanks, Forester." Jonas opened the door and turned back to Cole. "Oh, and one more thing. No bachelor party. It'll be too obvious. I can't risk Ava finding out."

Before Crys had come along, Cole would've ignored Jonas and found a way to host a party of the century, complete with top-notch strippers and top-shelf booze. But now he didn't seem to find much interest in half-naked, strange women and lap dances. The only woman he wanted to see in all her glory was the woman he had the privilege of seeing last night.

"If that's what you want."

"Don't look so disappointed. If you really want to have

some kind of bachelor party, we can throw one after the wedding."

"A bachelor party where the man of the hour isn't a bachelor anymore? Yeah, that sounds like a great idea, McKinley."

Chapter Seventeen

While Jonas was busy talking to Crys about his surprise wedding plans, Cole saddled his horse, Jail, and two others for the morning cow-calf check. It was early fall, and a time for transitioning from cowboy to midwife. Every successful rancher knew that each newborn calf played a vital part in the longevity of the business. From the time it dropped to the day it was weaned in spring, the calves required close monitoring in order to turn a profit. Not only did Jonas and Cole have to ensure that their cow-calf operation survived the harsh winters, they had to protect their investment from the many predatory animals that inhabited the area as well.

Most of the herd grazed in the open meadow, but after Cole counted heads, he found that a handful of mama cows were unaccounted for. A missing cow meant one of two things: she'd gone off to birth her calf in privacy, or she'd run into trouble with a hungry carnivore. With that in mind, he packed both his rifle and the identification tags necessary to earmark a calf with its mama.

It was best to tag calves within the first twenty-four hours of dropping. At that time, calves are still a little disoriented and often walking on wobbly legs. They're unable to run, and easier to handle as they're captured, tagged, and vaccinated. Sometimes, the risks in such a task prove just as dangerous as fending off a grizzly, especially when dealing with an overprotective mother cow.

No matter what the hazard, Cole enjoyed this time of year the most. Between hearing the bawl of a ridiculously cute calf and riding the range surrounded by colorful autumn foliage, he felt most at peace.

"So, how'd it go last night, Forester?" Rod asked as he sidled up next to Cole. "You know, with Ava's hot barrel racing friend?"

Cole's sense of tranquility suddenly just took a crap. "It went fine."

He probably should've known better than to think Rod would mind his own business, but where Crys was concerned, he took less of a liking to Rod's prying. So, he changed subjects quickly. "Just so you know, we should have a few mamas dropping calves today. You got your lariat with you? The light one?"

Rod raised it up for Cole to see and hung it on his saddle horn. As the two men mounted up, Cole hoped that

Rod would lose interest in small talk. He preferred peace and quiet to mindless drivel any day, especially when the conversation involved Crys.

"Hey, I hear congratulations are in order," Rod initiated.

Cole had no idea what his hired hand was referring to. "Come again?"

"You're McKinley's best man, right?"

"Oh yeah. Right. Best man."

"Jonas pulled me and Brody aside last night after you left and told us about his plans for a surprise wedding over at your place. It's sure going to be a hog-killin' time hitching those two love birds together after all these years. I only hope Brody can pull this off. He never was good at lying. Look how well he kept his love for Olivia a secret."

Cole adjusted his cowboy hat, wishing Jonas would hurry up. Rod's idle chatter was grating on his last nerve. He didn't know why, as he normally never had a problem with Rod. It probably had a lot to do with the fact that Rod took too much of a liking to Crys.

"Speaking of secrets," Rod continued. "I figure I'll let you in on one of mine. Especially since you've got that no-friends-and-family thing."

Cole's heart slowed at the mention of his rule.

"I'm sure you know where I'm going with this," Rod

prefaced with a wink. "But I've got the hots for ol' blondie."

Cole bit his tongue. "You don't say."

"Oh, yeah. I can't shake her from my mind. I was hoping to ask her out."

Suddenly, Cole wasn't the least bit worried about Rod moving in on his turf. Knowing that Crys wasn't so gentle in the feelings department, he thought it might be entertaining to watch Rod crash and burn. "You better bring your A game if you want a date with her."

Rod threw his head back and laughed. "When it comes to the ladies, you've got to know how to pour on the charm."

"Is that so?" Cole muttered, crossing his wrists over the horn of his saddle.

Rod circled Cole's horse in a cocky display of showmanship. "Here she comes now. Watch and learn, old man."

Cole didn't know what was funnier, the fact that Rod called him old when there was only two years between them, or that Rod thought he could score with Crys. Ready to watch the guy make a spectacle of himself, Cole reined his horse to face the entertainment.

Jail nickered at the approach of Crys's horse, and Jericho whinnied back. As Jonas and Crys approached from inside the barn, Cole wondered why she had saddled so soon. The trail tours didn't start for another three hours.

She wore a straight face and a tight pair of jeans. Despite the fact that she hardly made eye contact with him, she still looked as beautiful as a golden summer day in July.

"Morning, Ms. Crystal," Rod drawled out. "And to what do we owe the pleasure of your company this fine morning?"

"Jonas said Ava's got a light load for trail riders today. Care if I tag along?"

"We don't mind at all, Ms. Crystal. Mount your cute little butt on up there."

Jonas and Cole exchanged looks. Cole almost felt sorry for Rod.

"Mr. Galven," Crys called out starkly. "There's two things you should know about me. Number one, I despise the name Crystal."

Rod's smile disappeared. "Yes, ma'am."

"And two. Sweet talk never works on me."

Crys mounted Jericho and reined him away, giving Rod the cold shoulder and a clear view of her horse's hind end.

Jonas said nothing as he, too, mounted up. Cole on the other hand, couldn't hold his tongue as well as his friend. He trotted up next to Rod and patted his back.

"Way to go, young 'un. You certainly taught this old

man a thing or two. By the way, how's that foot taste?"

****

It was easy for Crys to forget all about Rod Galven when she had Cole Forester riding next to her. Men like Rod always had to prove themselves worthy via tireless bragging and artificial charm, whereas cowboys like Cole exuded confidence and appeal without any effort at all.

Throughout most of the journey across the open range, Cole hardly said a lick. He seemed more preoccupied with his surroundings than sneaking glances her way. Little did he know his aloofness captivated her about as much as when he walked out his bathroom in nothing but a towel the night before.

Try as she might, nothing could erase that splendid memory from her mind. And she was shocked at how often that image crept into her head, even when preoccupied with something as crucial as locating a handful of missing mama cows. Never before had one cowboy affected her so much.

What surprised her more was the distance the first mama cow had covered to birth her calf. The sheen of her Angus black coat shone like ebony silk under the morning sun. Steam rose from the back of her newborn calf lying in the grass, telling of its recent delivery into this world. It bawled and tried to stand, only to fail. The mother, prone to do almost anything to protect her vulnerable calf, stared and never left its side.

"All right, Cole," Jonas said calmly as he took out a small notepad and pen from his breast pocket. "You're up. This is cow number 0516. You'll have to let me know its gender when you get up there. I can't tell with it lying down."

"Got it."

Crys watched Cole dismount with a syringe, an ear tag, and a tag applicator from within his saddle bad. A pang of fear for the man she cared about struck her like a double-barrel kick to the chest. "You're going to vaccinate and tag this calf with its mama right there? Are you crazy?"

Cole ignored her and walked slowly toward the pair who waited along the tree line. Crys glanced at Rod, who sat silent on his horse with a lariat in hand. Jonas held pen to paper, neither moving a muscle.

"Aren't we supposed to help Cole? Shouldn't we lasso Mom or something before he does this?"

Jonas shushed her. "It's best for everyone to keep the stress of this process to a minimum. Cole's got this down to a science. It only takes a few seconds as long as everything goes right. Some people use gates, some use cages attached to a four-wheeler. But we've found that it works better if Mom isn't separated from her calf."

Crys swallowed hard, watching Cole approach with tentative steps. She was glad that Jonas explained everything to her as it unfolded.

"See how's he's keeping the calf between him and the mom. Even if she wants to charge, she won't do anything that would ultimately hurt her calf."

Crys watched in awe as Cole reached out for the youngster, flipped it over on its side, and held it to the ground with his knee. As he calmly tagged its left ear, the mother took a step forward and sniffed her bawling calf.

"Oh God." Crys prepared for the worst.

"He's all right," Jonas soothed. "Mom is watchful, but she's not crazy. Now see how he tagged the left ear? That means it's a female. And the number on the tag matches her mama's so we know who belongs with whom in case they ever get separated. Later on in spring, she'll be given a shot of RB51 for Brucellosis, and we'll add a metal clip in her right ear to indicate she's been vaccinated."

Crys held her breath as she saw Cole pocket the applicator and uncap the syringe with his teeth. The calf bawled again when he inserted the needle, and Mom lowered her head in a defensive posture and blew snot. Within seconds, Cole lifted the calf to her feet and stroked her hide. The calf took a wobbly step, and Cole slowly backed up, keeping an eye on the mother. Once the cow realized her calf was no worse for wear, Cole returned to his horse unharmed.

Crys blew out a tremendous sigh of relief as he mounted his horse beside her. "That was amazing."

Cole removed his hat and swiped his brow. "This coming from a girl whose brothers ride bulls for a living. It's not that impressive compared to them."

"Yes it is. They have several full-grown bullfighters with years of experience watching their backs. The only thing between you and a serious ass-kicking is a helpless sixty-pound calf."

"They don't always cooperate, do they, Cole?" Jonas tucked the notepad away and smiled as if he recalled an instance when one such cow had gotten the best of him. "Cole's been slammed to the ground and smeared across the field more times than he'd care to admit. One year, he landed in the hospital with a broken rib and a sprained ankle."

The more Crys heard, the more she admired Cole for his bravery, not to mention his cow-whispering skills. "Are you the only one who can do this?"

"Nah. Jonas does it too," Cole said flatly. "He's the one who taught me."

"So, how do you decide who's risking their neck for

the day?" Crys didn't mean to ask so many questions. She was unaccustomed to this way of life and found every aspect of Wyoming ranch living far more appealing than racing a six-shooter horse around three barrels.

"Every day is as different as whiskey and tea," Jonas explained. "Sometimes we take turns. Sometimes we don't. It all depends on the day and how successful it proves to be."

"Are we going to keep talking this into the dirt?" Cole asked Jonas. "Or are we gonna get something done?"

Jonas gave his friend a peculiar look of interest. "You got some place to be?"

"Yeah. Some dickhead wants his wedding at my barn, and I'm a little pressed for time."

Jonas laughed and urged his horse forward, leading the pack. "Well, I'm sure that dickhead really appreciates that his asshole best man's taking it so seriously."

As they scooted along, looking for the next missing cow, Crys appreciated the lessons she'd learned out on the range. Not only did she witness the behind-the-scenes work that went into running a cattle farm, she also observed Cole at his finest.

He was both diligent and ornery, yet gentle and patient, a jumble of traits she'd not seen in any cowboy before. Between the way he touched and kissed her last night to the way he treated his dog and handled day-old calves under the protective watch of intimidating mama cows, Cole was a prize catch.

Chapter Eighteen

Fall-calving season was in full swing at the McKinley ranch. For the next few weeks, Cole, Jonas, and the Galven brothers monitored the herd of pregnant cows on a daily basis and kept detailed records as the calves dropped. Out of the fifty bred, forty-nine delivered without complication and two gave birth to twins, proving the trial run with the new bull successful. Overall, they tagged and vaccinated over fifty calves, with two-thirds castrated for next year's rodeos. The rest would be raised as heifers for breeding or sold for quality Angus beef.

Also during this time, Crys and Ava closed down the trail tours, and turned thirty horses out to pasture until winter snowfall deemed otherwise. Along with the hundreds of cattle roaming the McKinley ranch, the horses ate meadow grass for as long as the weather permitted. It was considered a successful grazing season if ranchers could make it without feeding hay until after late December. According to the *Farmers' Almanac*, things didn't look promising.

With only a month left to prepare for the nuptials, everyone worked full bore to help Jonas pull off the wedding of Ava's dreams. Jonas and Cole labored every morning to relocate their farm equipment, stash the extra hay behind Cole's barn, and tarp it down. The Galven brothers took care of the daily cattle responsibilities, which included riding out with rifles to protect the herd from Wyoming's predators.

Rhonda, being Ava's computer-savvy assistant, ordered and mailed the invitations and set up a Pinterest account so Ava, without her realizing, could narrow down the details of her perfect fall wedding. Little did Ava know, the inspirational board became a landing point through which Jonas could secretly purchase all the items necessary for flower arrangements, bouquets, table decorations, and lighting. Even the dress Ava picked out was saved there.

Two weeks later, everything had shipped to Cole's address, and Ava's gown was set to ship to Rhonda's, where she could alter it ahead of time. Jonas assured Crys that Rhonda knew Ava's dimensions to a T, as she'd sewn a skimpy lingerie piece a few months ago. By the look on Jonas's face, Crys knew there was something more to that story, but didn't ask.

Day by day, everything fell into place, with Ava none

the wiser. Lucky for Crys, Ava wanted a simple wedding, and most of the pieces necessary to pull together a country-western theme were already at her disposal in Cole's barn. In the midst of cleaning it out, she and Cole found several wagon wheels, a few old wooden barrels, rusty barbed wire, and many mason jars.

In the weeks leading up to the big day, Crys continued to help Ava with the farm chores in the mornings, and then drove to Cole's in the evenings. Together, they swept out cobwebs, hung lights, and set up hay bales inside for seating. To her surprise, Cole even helped her with the table decorations. There was something extremely cute about a rough and rugged cowboy hot-gluing daisies and burlap strips to mason jar candles.

Though she and Cole spent lots of time working alone together, laughing and sneaking kisses at every turn, they never really had a chance to be intimate again. But it wasn't because they didn't try. It seemed that every time they succumbed to temptation, someone showed up at Cole's. When coupled with the fact that Crys had to leave by nightfall so Ava wouldn't question her whereabouts, they were about as sexually frustrated as two people could get.

At the end of week four, with nothing left to string up, hot glue, or rivet, Cole couldn't take it any longer. He threw her over his shoulder, spanked her butt playfully, and carried her to the barn.

Crys braced her draped body by pushing off his lower back. "Where are we going?"

"Where no one can find us."

They saddled up Jail and Elvis, an extra horse he'd long retired, and rode out to a remote place on his ranch. There, she caught a glimpse of the cowboy outside the dutiful rancher.

As she rode abreast of him, she gazed out at the rugged scenery before her. A canvas of bright blue sky backdropped a grove of golden aspens exploding with color along the edges of a white pine forest. In the distance, a vista of mountainous peaks and grassy bluffs molded into the stark terrain of Wyoming's treeless badlands.

The contrast of that breathtaking landscape reminded her of the inexplicable cowboy seated on his fifteen-three-hand quarter horse. He was hot, he was cold, and half the time he kept her guessing. She only wished she understood him better.

It was obvious he felt something for her, or he would've given up this fling weeks ago. But what did he want from her that was worth pursuing?

Companionship?

Commitment?

Did he ever look toward the future?

And if he did, was she there?

Regardless of Cole's ambiguity, she couldn't kid herself any longer. Though she came to Meeteetse without the desire to find a man, she discovered a whole new breed of cowboy in Cole Forester that she couldn't stand to lose.

****

Cole steered Jail up an incline and into a thicket of pines to the east. Crys followed with Sammy trailing right beside her. Several paces in, Cole stopped his horse at a small clearing and peered over his shoulder. The look on Crys's face was priceless.

"We're camping? Are you serious? When did you do this?"

"Last night, after you left."

He swung his right leg over Jail's neck and dismounted in one leap. He considered the four-man tent he'd staked on a bed of pine needles, the pile of wood he stacked beside a ringlet of stones, and the Coleman lantern he paired with a cooler full of beer. Was it all too presumptuous on his part?

"It's perfect," she said. "Everything is. The location. The company. How we got here."

"I figured you'd like that."

Cole tied the horses to a picket line he'd also secured ahead of time between two tall evergreens.

"What I really like is this incredible view." Crys regarded the deep valley below through the curtain of coniferous tree limbs. "You sure you don't want to sell just a parcel?"

It would be a cold day in hell before Cole sold one acre of his two-thousand-acre paradise. But with Crys, the idea of sharing his land with a woman who appreciated its raw beauty somehow didn't seem so crazy.

Was that even possible?

It amazed him how easily she roped his heart into submission. If anyone had told him that one day he'd be broke and hog-tied, he wouldn't have believed it possible from a woman who once held him at gunpoint. Though Crys had never forced anything from him beyond a fling, she had him contemplating if they were destined to become more than friends.

As scary as it all sounded, he was more terrified by the possibility that Crys might not feel the same way. She was a restless spirit with a mile-high heap of pride, who'd left her family to strike out on her own. The chances of her wanting more from a hardheaded, apathetic cattle rancher were slim to none.

Tucking his thoughts into the deep recesses of his

mind, he reached for Crys on her horse and set her on her feet.

"You okay?" she asked, measuring him. "You look a little frazzled. Did the mention of selling your land freak you out or something? 'Cause I was only kidding."

Cole laughed it off. "'Course you were. And I'm fine. I'm just…"

His words trailed off when he felt her grasp on his forearm. He wanted to tell her how every rule he'd ever had about women and dating was fast becoming a thing of the past.

She stepped into his space and gazed into his eyes. "Do I detect a little nervousness?"

He tried to play it cool. "No…" *Liar.* "Well, maybe a little."

Her smile soothed him, making him feel as if he had nothing to be ashamed of for wanting more than just the friends-with-benefits arrangement.

"What's going on in that head of yours, Cole? Are we moving too fast for your liking?"

"I can see why you'd think that. But actually, I'm trying to figure out what's in your head. I don't feel like I know you all that well. And I want to. I want to know what makes you happy. What made you give up on your career. Why you only talk about your father and brothers and rarely your mother."

As soon as he mentioned her family, Crys blinked repeatedly as if taken aback.

"Sorry, we don't have to talk about that if—"

"No, it's okay," she said, stepping back. "I don't mind. What do you want to know?"

Cole walked over to the cooler and twisted off the tops of two beers. As he handed Crys a bottle, he smiled. "I want to know everything you feel comfortable telling me."

Chapter Nineteen

Crys stared at the warm crackling fire before her, snuggling into Cole's embrace as they sat within the swaddle of sleeping bags draped around their shoulders. She felt an unexpected sense of serenity in sharing the story of how her mother died when Crys was just a teen. Though she'd never spoken of it at length with anyone before, she was glad he'd asked. It proved to her that he wanted something more from this fling than just a physical relationship. What's more, she felt a deeper connection with him because he too took the time to share things about his family that most people didn't know either.

As she thought about how the course of their conversation had taken them to her career and what she wanted out of life, it eventually led back to Cole and how they'd met on Highway 120. She never thought that reminiscing over the forgotten past and yarning the hours away would be so enjoyable. Perhaps it was the seclusion, or the crickets and the stars that surrounded them in the middle of nowhere. All she knew was that amid the quiet solitude of their secret hiding place, she felt completely at home.

She glanced around, taking in the tranquil stillness of the evening. Sammy lay at Cole's feet, while Jail and Elvis slept standing up, as most horses did.

"Are you cold?" Cole asked, tugging her closer. "I can throw another log on the fire."

She took pleasure in his subtle thoughtfulness and warmed her hands against the warm bare skin of his stomach beneath his flannel shirt. Touching him brought her an undeniable feeling of greed she'd never felt before. She wanted him all to herself and couldn't begin to fathom the thought of another woman with him. "Are you always this considerate of the women you date?"

"You forget. I don't date much."

"Yes, but I know I'm not the first woman you've ever had."

He took a sip of his beer, pondering. "You're the first woman I've ever brought *here*. Ever brought on my land, period. So, to answer your question...no. I guess I'm not all that considerate of women. That's more Jonas's style."

She spun to face him. "So, why are you considerate with me?"

Cole laughed as he shook his head. "I don't know why.

With you, I just strive for good manners. Can't you just take my word for it?"

"I could, but where would the fun be in that? Besides, I love that you've finally opened up to me."

"How do I explain something I can't figure out myself?" He reached up and brushed back her hair, contemplating as he stared into her eyes. "This is all so new to me, Angel. I can't put into words how you make me feel. All I know is I'm perfectly happy when I'm with you, and I hate when you have to leave."

Crys felt her heart swell with Cole's confession. Like him, she loved the brief moments they'd had together and looked so forward to the next one down the road. Whether it was spent working alongside him in the barn or sneaking off to steal a kiss from his beautiful mouth, every opportunity to be in his company was the highlight of her day.

"I hope you know I feel the same way," she said.

"You do?"

The look of surprise on his handsome face was almost childlike. "How could you not know that, Cole? Because of you, I've not spent a single day looking for a place to live, and while that should concern me on so many levels, I don't seem to care. I've put spending time with you above my own priorities."

She watched Cole's expression change from dreamy to solemn.

"I kind of forgot that you're..."

"Homeless," she joked.

He furrowed his brow. "Yeah. That."

"Hey," Crys said, cradling his jaw. "It's not your fault. I'm a grown woman who's perfectly capable of getting in my truck and property-shopping any time I want. I just chose not to, or rather, I forget about it. If you're going to take the blame for anything, you can accept that you're my distraction."

A slow grin curved his lips. "I like being your distraction."

"Yeah, well, can you please distract me from the fact that I should be getting back to my trailer before Ava wonders where I am?"

Cole leaned in and kissed her lips in a way that diverted her every thought from leaving his side. From the heat in his gaze to the woodsy smell of his skin, she focused on the man who was totally worth ditching everything for.

"It's working," she baited.

His open palm slid past her cheek and into her hair. She felt the strong points of his fingertips grip the nape of her neck and pull her in close for a deeper, more passionate kiss. His tongue swept into her mouth, gliding along hers in potent, possessive strokes. Kissing Cole was like shooting Southern Comfort whiskey, sweet with a rush of fire burning deep in her chest.

"Stay the night with me," he whispered against her lips.

Still half-intoxicated by his kiss, his touch, she could barely think beyond his request. "What about Ava? And Jonas. They'll worry."

"Text them something. Tell them you're fine but you're not coming home."

He dipped to her throat and sucked on the skin tight against the cords in her neck, then bit down tenderly. The ache she'd become accustomed to feeling every time she was with him grew stronger with each sinful thing he did to her.

"And where do I say I am?"

"Tell them you've found some cowboy in town. That way you're not lying." Cole's hand, hot and callused, slipped beneath her shirt. "It's not out of your character, is it?"

It was definitely not out of her character. Before Cole, she occasionally hooked up with an available cowboy for a night of fun and drinks. She could even admit to sometimes indulging in a little casual sex as a stress relief given her once-intense training schedule and her overbearing family members. "I guess Ava's known me to hook up a time or two."

"So, text her," he whispered heatedly. "Spend the night with me, Angel. Tell me I didn't set this tent up for nothing."

There was no point trying to deny herself the pleasure of being with Cole, especially when no one was around to disturb them. She was only kidding herself if she thought she could resist that look of restless hunger in his eyes. Everything about him, including his persistence, tempted her to concede. If Cole wasn't worried about Ava and Jonas finding out, then why should she?

Crys slipped out of his arms, stepped over Sammy, and sauntered her way toward the tent. "If you'll excuse me, I have a call to make."

Crys unzipped the tent and fumbled to find her cell in her jacket. Outside, she heard Cole command Sammy to stay seconds before Cole burst through the opening wrapped in the bundle of sleeping bags. He tackled her on the mattress, and she loved the way his deep laughter mingled with hers as she tried to type her vague message to Ava. It became increasingly difficult to text with Cole kissing her neck and shoulder from behind as he pulled off her coat.

When her sentence was complete, she paused and showed him the screen of her smartphone. "Last chance, Cole. You sure you want to do this?"

Cole looked up and read the text to Ava. He smiled as he reached over and pressed Send. "I'm sure."

He rolled her to her back and climbed on top, concentrating on nothing but her face. His dark eyes never looked as intense as they did right then, and she wondered what this magnificent, unpredictable man could possible say next.

"Now that we finally have all night to be together, I'm going to take my time getting to know every fraction of your beautiful figure. I want to memorize every curve," he stated, running his hands along her waist and hips. "How's that for opening up?"

He leaned in slowly and pressed his mouth to hers, blessing her with the most heartfelt kiss she'd ever gotten from him. In his gaze, where she used to see lust and hunger, she now saw sincerity and tenderness—proof that he intended to make slow, reverent love with her.

Crys tossed her phone aside and wrapped her arms around her wicked cowboy's neck for the newfangled, next go-round.

Chapter Twenty

Crys pulled up to the McKinley ranch the following morning with the blissful memory of waking up in Cole's arms. Seeing his handsome face the moment she'd opened her eyes had her floating so high, she worried she'd be hard-pressed to hide her emotions where everyone else was concerned.

While she and Cole had certainly crossed a bridge in their relationship, he was still set on hiding it from those closest to him. In the beginning, she thought it no big deal to keep the fling under wraps, as that was all it would likely be. But now, things had changed—at least for her. Cole was no longer just a sexy, brooding cowboy she had to have. He was a friend, a lover, and man she was falling deeply in love with.

Struck by her own true feelings, she also came to acknowledge that matters of the heart didn't so easily influence Cole. He'd been a self-proclaimed bachelor all his life and getting him to accept that a committed relationship, out in the open, wasn't his doom, would take a miracle.

As she parked her truck and hopped out, she caught a glimpse of Ava turning over a wheelbarrow full of manure in the pit outside the barn. She knew it would take another miracle to dodge her friend's concern for where she'd been all night. By the look on Ava's face, she started to regret the extra hours she'd spent eating breakfast with Cole after they rode back to his house and unsaddled the horses.

"Good morning," Crys said tentatively.

Ava gave her a stern look, the kind her father would give her when he didn't approve of something that interfered with her training. "It's almost afternoon."

"I know. And I'm sorry if I made you worry, Ava. I just needed a break from—"

"You're a grown woman," Ava interrupted, "and you can do what you want. Just because you're temporarily living here doesn't mean you have to report to me like I'm some parental figure."

Despite Ava's reassuring words, Crys didn't feel all that comforted by them. To her, it felt a little disconcerting that Ava left the subject mildly open-ended. "Thanks, I guess."

"What I'm trying to say is that you can come and go as you please, but just at least be cautious when meeting new people. I don't want to see you get hurt."

Hearing the distress in Ava's voice, Crys wished she

could ease her friend's mind and tell her exactly where she'd been all night and with whom. If Ava knew Cole had been the cowboy she'd found in town, Ava would be relieved—and extremely happy since she'd wanted to get them together from the beginning.

She rode the fence with telling Ava about her little secret love affair. They'd been friends for more than twenty years, and she knew she could trust Ava to keep it to herself.

But she'd also made a solemn promise to Cole. Not tarnishing the trust he had in her was more important.

"Would it make you feel any better if I told you I had a really nice time with this guy?"

Ava's interested spiked. "You did?"

"So much that I think I may have found someone compatible with me."

Ava smiled, wrapping her arm around Crys. "Really? Wow, this is news." Ava's grin slipped. "Just please tell me you used protection."

Crys drew back. "What makes you think I had sex with him?"

"Please," Ava said, batting her hand once. "You're talking to me as if I don't know you. Look at you. You're glowing."

Crys brought her hand up to her face as if she could

feel the radiance on her skin. "Is it that obvious?"

Jonas came around the corner carrying two buckets of grain for his cattle. "Yes. It's obvious you've had sex. And I don't even know you that well."

"Jonas," Ava scolded.

"What? She asked."

"Yes, but you were eavesdropping."

Jonas cracked up. "Look who's calling the kettle black."

Ava jammed her fists on her hips. "Really? That again?"

Crys put her hand on Ava's shoulder as Jonas walked away laughing. "It's fine. I don't care that he was listening. Evidently I couldn't hide it anyway."

Ava's smile returned. "So, who is this cowboy you met last night? Would I know him?"

Crys swallowed, unsure of how to answer. As she beat her brain trying to come up with a response that wouldn't be a lie, the cowboy himself pulled in the drive.

Her stomach churned, but she lifted her chin in a display of confidence. She couldn't help the sidelong glances she gave him, or the race of her heart as she watched him exit his truck. He strolled up to the barn, with Sammy at his heels, in the most casual way. Not a bit of reluctance plagued his stride. With his shoulders back and his chest out, he met the two of them as impassive as a copper head on a penny.

"Are you going to tell me, or do I have to guess?" Ava asked.

Cole stopped short and bent to pat his loyal dog at his feet. "Guess what?"

"The name of the cowboy that Crys spent the night with last night."

Crys watched Cole's brow lift and his Adam's apple bob, but he didn't say a word. She couldn't tell if he was worried or agitated.

"It's unimportant what his name is, and I doubt Cole, here, cares to know."

Ava slugged his arm. "He should care because he missed out on his chance. See? That could've been you. But no, you have rules."

"I *do* have rules," Cole finally stated. "And lucky for me, it keeps conversations like this from mounting."

Ava hugged Cole around the waist. "You know I was only playing."

"I know. And I should be used to it by now."

"Yes, you should. If anyone has ever had your back around this place, it's me."

Cole smirked and bowed out, joining Jonas in the routine chore of feeding cattle. Sammy sat patiently at

Crys's feet, and the three of them eyed Cole as he picked up two buckets and scooped grain from the bin.

Ava clicked her tongue. "There goes one stubborn mule. I swear, all he needs to do is find the right woman and he'd be right as rain. Sure wish it could've been you," she said, slapping Crys's back. "Oh well. No sense filling the pit when the calf's already drowned."

****

After Cole finished feeding, he made his way to the barn, looking for Crys. He tried not to care about the discussion she and Ava were having when he pulled in, but his curiosity was killing him. He liked the idea of telling everyone that he and Crys had been having an ongoing relationship since they'd first met, but he wasn't quite sure he was ready to make that leap.

Yes, last night was amazing.

And yes, she was the most extraordinary woman he'd ever met.

But the heat of their secret fling had spiraled into emotions he swore he'd never let himself feel so quickly, and the thought of tearing down the first good thing he ever had with a woman scared the living hell out of him.

He'd be a liar if he didn't admit he felt something for

Crys. Was it the start of a growing affection? Or maybe something stronger?

Cole took off his hat and swiped his brow. The thought of that four-letter L word had him quaking in his boots. It was preposterous to even think he might love Crys, as he only knew her for little over a month.

With Jonas and Ava out of sight, he needed to see her again, to hold her, to press her close and taste her kiss.

Peering into each stall, he searched and whispered for her. "Crys? Crys? Where are you?"

Crys stepped out of Jericho's stall with a manure rake in hand. Sammy followed and wagged his tail in delight.

Before she could answer, Cole swooped in and gathered her in his arms. Backing her into an empty stall, he kissed her hard, much harder than he planned. She dropped the rake and wrapped her arms around him, matching his fervor with her own.

She tasted so good, possibly even better than she did this morning when she left his house. He had trouble pulling her close enough. He spun her around and crushed her against the stall, sandwiching her between him and solid galvanized steel bars.

"Cole! You in here?"

Cole froze mid-kiss, and Crys stopped breathing.

It was Jonas.

FALLING FOR FORESTER: (COLE & CRYS)

They couldn't hide, as Sammy would surely give them away, and they couldn't run. They were totally trapped with no escape.

Cole pushed off the rail and gawked at Crys in wide-eyed alarm. At the sound of Jonas's boot steps, Cole panicked. He shut the stall door and shoved her to a squat at his feet as he leaned forward. Propping his elbows on the wooden edge, he hung out the feed door and answered back. "I'm in here."

He cleared his throat and tried not to think about the precarious position he'd put Crys in to hide her. No doubt, her face tarried mere inches from his groin, and that very image presented him with a complexity all its own.

"Oh, there you are," Jonas said, as he approached and patted Sammy's head. "Hey, have you—" Jonas clammed up the moment he laid eyes on Cole in the stall. "What are you doing?"

"I'm taking a piss. Do you mind?" Cole reached down and pretended to fiddle with his zipper.

Jonas quickly backed up and averted his gaze. "Seriously?"

"Horses do it in here. Why can't I?" Cole glanced down between his legs. Seeing Crys sent a jolt of excitement through him. He fought to keep his emotions at bay with Jonas only a few feet away. He tore his gaze from

Crys and slanted his upper body back over the stall. "What is it you want, McKinley?"

"I'm looking for Crys. Have you seen her?"

Cole hesitated. "Ah, no... What do you need her for?"

Jonas took a glance over his shoulder and back at Cole. "With Ava in the house, I wanted to get with you and Crys and see how everything was going for this Saturday."

Cole glanced again at Crys for a split second. "What about Saturday?"

"Uh, it's my wedding day."

"Oh, right. Sure. Yes. Everything's ready to go."

Jonas crossed his arms. "You about done in there?"

"No..." Cole yielded, tilting his head to the side. "Not quite."

"What the hell did you drink this morning, a whole pot of coffee?"

"So it would seem."

"Okay, Cole, it's getting a little uncomfortable talking to you while you're taking a leak, so I'll make this brief. Ava's leaving early Friday morning to pick up her son at the airport in Jackson Hole. She thinks Sawyer's coming to town for his birthday. I need you and Crys to be at my house so we can finalize arrangements for the wedding. Rhonda's coming about nine. Can you make it?"

"Sure thing."

Jonas started to back out of the barn. "Well, if you see Crys, will you tell her for me?"

"You betcha."

Jonas turned to leave with a scowl on his face. "When you're done, head up to the house. Lunch is ready."

As soon as Jonas stepped out of sight, Cole stood up straight and pulled Crys to a stand. "That was close."

"It was," she agreed. "It was only a couple inches from my face."

Cole chuckled. "That's not what I meant. I was talking about Jonas."

"I know what you were talking about. I was just joking. I still can't believe Jonas had no idea. You know how close we came to ruining our secret? Crazy close."

Cole cradled her face and brushed his thumbs across her cheeks flushed with heat. As he gazed at the beautiful angel in his hands, he saw for the first time an innocence where he used to see a devil-may-care desire. "You know what's crazy? I feel like I can't remember my life before you. All I know is you. All I *need* is you."

Chapter Twenty-one

Five days came and went, and Crys was still floating on air from the words Cole had used to describe his feelings that fateful Sunday afternoon. Men like Cole didn't often divulge that kind of stuff. But she also knew Cole was not a liar. If he felt the need to say something, it was the honest-to-God truth.

Although he admitted to needing her, he still hadn't fessed up to his friends. Jonas was unaware of anything going on between her and Cole, and Ava was clearly oblivious to everything, including her fiancé's surprise wedding plans.

While Ava was at the airport picking up her son, she, Rhonda, and Cole sat around Jonas's kitchen table, ready to finalize the logistics of tomorrow's special day.

Crys sipped her coffee and struggled to keep her eyes off Cole as Jonas ended a call he made to Brody. He pocketed his cell and smiled.

"It's official. Brody said Olivia would be honored to

sing at the wedding. She's here for one more week before she heads back to Nashville so the timing's perfect." He looked to Rhonda now. "Where are we with the music?"

"Rod said he spoke with Jethro—he's the owner of the Wagon Wheel," she spelled out for Crys before continuing, "and he offered to let us borrow his equipment for the weekend. That includes the soundboard, speakers, and mics. He also said he'd be willing to set it all up for us, and DJ the reception afterward if we wanted."

"Tell him he's hired," Jonas said, "and cut him a check."

Rhonda marked her spreadsheet and brought up the next item on her list. "Crys, how are the decorations going?"

Crys set her mug down, and exchanged glances with Cole. "We finished the table decorations sometime last week, and they're all in boxes ready to go."

"What about tables and chairs for eating? Do we need to rent some?"

"Actually, with all the extra hay we needed to remove from Cole's barn, he and I came up with a great idea for tables and seating using the bales. Here, I took a picture of it."

Crys pulled out her cell and showed off their creative innovation using the bales. A provisional tabletop made of two sheets of sanded and stained oak sat upon three sets of double-high stacked bales. A white cloth runner and candles dressed up the center, while mason jars stuffed with silverware and alternating blue and red handkerchiefs charmed each place setting with a casual-chic western motif. A single row of bales set end to end made up the benches on either side. Foot-wide planks ran down the middle for both comfort and added elegance.

"That is the cutest thing I've ever seen!" Rhonda exclaimed. "Ava will love this!"

Jonas nodded as he stared at the DIY ensemble. "That she will."

"Oh, and along with the pretty tables," Crys added as she swiped to the next picture, "Cole built a beautiful pine arbor for you and Ava to stand under as you say your vows."

Jonas spread his thumb and pointer finger on the screen to enlarge the image and looked at it closely. "Nice work, Forester. I'm impressed."

"Good, because it's your wedding gift."

"What's even more impressive," Crys explained further, unable to contain her admiration for the man who went the extra mile for his best friend, "is that all the lumber Cole used came straight off the McKinley ranch."

"Another gift from me to you," he added flatly.

"Well, I'll be damned, Cole. I didn't know you to be sentimental."

Jonas might not have known, but Crys had seen it firsthand. With each long stroke Cole had made to hand-sand every piece of wood to perfection, she witnessed his dedication to those he cared about most. She even called to mind the special night she camped with him on his land. Undoubtedly, there was more to Cole than met the eye.

"Now realize, Jonas, that's one of ten tables, none of which are set up yet in case it rained between then and now. If Brody and Rod can be there first thing in the morning, we should be able to kick them out in no time."

Rhonda marked her list again. "I'll make sure they're there to help. Anything else that needs setting up?"

"Not that I can think of. The hay bales we've designated for seating inside the barn during the ceremony are all in place, and so is the arbor."

"What about the lighting?" Jonas asked.

"Swipe the screen," Crys directed on her cell. The next picture displayed a canopy of tiny white lights crisscrossing the beams in the barn and down around each post. Even the arbor was strung with lights, along with rusty horseshoes, white daisies, and decorative dried branches. "What do you think?"

Jonas shook his head in wonder. "You and Cole have

definitely outdone yourselves. This is better than I could've ever imagined. Ava's going to be so pleased."

"Let's just hope she's pleased with the alterations I've done on the dress she picked out," Rhonda said, then pointed to Cole. "Can I bring it by your place tonight?"

"Wait, what?"

Crys saw the look of horror on Cole's face. He didn't seem to take kindly to the fact that something as feminine as a wedding dress would hang in his bachelor's pad.

"Since Ava won't have any idea she's about to get married, she has to get dressed somewhere, Cole."

He looked to Jonas now. "Ava has to get ready at my house?"

Jonas offered his friend a look of pity instead of an alternate solution. "I'm afraid so, buddy."

"We all have to," Rhonda said.

Cole's eyes widened, and his mouth fell open. "All of you? What does this mean? How many is that?"

"Calm yourself, Cole. It's just me and Crys. And then there's the bride of course. So, three."

Jonas laughed as Cole squeezed his eyes shut.

"Three women," he articulated with dread. "In my house. At one time."

"With makeup, and bras, and all kinds of frilly stuff," Rhonda added cruelly. "Maybe even a tampon or two."

Crys imagined Cole was stricken with absolute trepidation as he pictured his rustic, manly home defiled by girly accessories and feminine hygiene products. She almost felt sorry for the poor guy.

"Don't worry, Cole. I'll make sure it's all cleaned up before the night's over. If it makes you feel any better, I'll be taking Ava into Cody tomorow morning to get a complete makeover at the salon, so when we return, we'll just have to slip on our dresses. She thinks we're just having a girl's day of pampering before we check out some houses I've had my eye on."

Rhonda checked off another item on her list. "Crys, I have your appointment set for nine a.m. at the Hair Affaire & 11th Street Spa. It's the first appointment of the day, so you shouldn't run into any delays. You and Ava are getting massages, manicures, hair, and makeup. I suggest you tell Ava to get her hair and makeup done like she'd want for her wedding as a practice run to make sure she likes it. Whatever it takes to get her to be bride-ready."

"Bride-ready. Got it."

"Wait, what do you mean houses you've had your eye on?" Cole asked, a little off the beaten path. He looked mildly confused that she intended to buy a house.

Crys was just as puzzled by his reaction. "You know I'm in the market for a house and some acreage. Granted, I haven't been able to look at anything because I've been with you most every day for the sake of this wedding, but yes, I'm still looking. I can't stay in my trailer below Jonas's barn forever."

Jonas let out a nervous laugh. "No, she cannot."

Though Cole hadn't said a word, Crys noticed a change in his composure and wasn't quite sure what to make of it. He knew that buying property was her main priority since she'd accepted a full-time job at the McKinley ranch, and she even recalled mentioning it the night they sat around a campfire. Despite that it had been moved to the back burner for time being, it was still the next step she had to take.

"Moving on," Rhonda said tentatively, "the caterer will arrive while the ceremony is taking place. Crys, did you and Cole designate a spot for serving food?"

Crys blinked and slipped out of her reverie. "Uh, yes. We cleaned up some barrels, and Cole stained another sheet of wood for the tabletop. Like the dinner tables, it just needs to be set up in the morning."

"Wonderful. And I'll make sure I'm there early to see to the place settings and mason jars." Rhonda marked her paper again and bit the tip of her pen. "Looks like the last thing on my list is the florist. I've had them create a few arrangements for the serving tables, and I'll put the bouquets and boutonnieres in Cole's fridge until Ava arrives. Cole, do you have room?"

Cole sat there, his eyes glazing over as he stared at his coffee cup.

"Cole?" Rhonda tried again. "Did you hear me?"

He looked up. "No, I didn't. Sorry."

Everyone stared at him, including Jonas. "She asked if you had room in your fridge for the girls' flowers. Are you all right?"

Cole stood up and glanced at the front door. "I'm fine. I just need some air. Are we finished here?"

Rhonda raised both hands, palms up. "We are as long as we have somewhere for the flowers to go and you have a nice tie and shirt to wear."

Cole waved it off. "I'll make room. And yes, I have a shirt and tie."

"Is it blue?" Rhonda asked. "Because you have to match Crys."

"Right. Blue. Whatever. Now if you'll excuse me, I have things I need to do."

****

Cole stepped outside and righted his cowboy hat on his head, thankful for the crisp morning air. Sammy jumped from his nap on the porch and met him at the stairs. Before he and his dog could make it halfway to his truck, Jonas came bursting out the door.

"Hey, wait up!"

Cole halted and sighed. He knew his friend all too well. *Why can't he let it ride?*

When Jonas met up with him, he crossed his arms and feigned indifference. "What's up?"

"You tell me." Jonas said, glancing over his shoulder at his house. "What the hell happened back there?"

"I don't know what you're talking about."

"Come on, Cole. We've been friends for way too long. Is there something going on between you and Crys that I don't know about? Aside from the usual tension, of course."

There was plenty going on between him and Crys, but none of it made a lick of sense. They had agreed on a secret fling with no strings attached, but he was tied in knots over the fact that he wanted more. He treasured his bachelor's life, but he hated waking up every morning without Crys in his bed. And now that he realized she was still set on finding her own place, he worried that maybe he'd taken too much of their secret relationship to heart.

Although he was dying to tell someone, he and Crys had never really talked about whether they were ready to come out in the open with it. She might be upset with him if he came clean without her permission.

"There's nothing going on, McKinley."

"You sure? 'Cause you looked pretty disappointed when Crys mentioned buying a house." Jonas searched his face for a clue. "Why wouldn't you want her to do that? Are you still having issues with the fact that she's decided to live in Meeteetse?"

"No." And that was the damned truth. He'd only have issues if she decided *not* to live there.

"So, what it is, Forester? You can tell me. You know it'll stay right here between us."

If Cole knew anything, it was Jonas's loyalty. Under pain of death, Jonas would always keep his word. "Look, it's no big deal. I just forgot that she was looking for a place to live, and it threw me for a loop."

Jonas laughed. "So, Ava did hear right when she overheard you saying you had feeling for Crys."

Cole stiffened as he recalled that epic night on Jonas's porch, the conversation that started this whole mess, and the earth-shattering kiss he'd shared with Crys to seal the deal. "*Had* feelings," Cole reiterated. "It's now a thing of the past. I've moved on. She's moved on. End of story."

"Does this have anything to do with the cowboy she met with last weekend?"

Ever since that weekend, Cole had been struggling to make sense of his emotions, feelings he didn't know how to categorize.

Did he want her? Yes.

Did he need her? Yes.

Did he love her? Who knew.

He'd never been in love, so the idea was as foreign to him as wearing a dress.

"It has everything to do with that, Jonas. And right now, I need a break. I've been working my ass off for you, and I need a little downtime. From you. From her. From everyone."

Jonas took a step back, and it seemed he knew he pushed too far. "Cole, I'm sorry. I've been so busy with trying to plan this wedding for Ava that I didn't even think about the work you've done for me."

Of all the things Cole felt as he stood there, guilt plagued him now. "I shouldn't have said it like that. I was happy to do it."

"No, no. I need to make this up to you. You and Crys both, because the truth is, I couldn't have pulled this off without you. Sure, Rhonda, took care of all the legwork and scheduling, thank the Lord, but you guys did more than any friend could expect." Jonas extended his hand. "From the bottom of my heart, Forester, I thank you."

Cole shook Jonas's hand in earnest, then pulled him into a manly hug. "Just don't ever get married again, you hear?"

Jonas laughed aloud and beat Cole's back with a couple of hard slaps. "I don't plan on it, trust me. This is it." Jonas's smile softened, and he regarded Cole with a look of sincerity. "She's the love of my life, you know that? Ever since I first met Ava, I knew I wanted to spend the rest of my days with her. You know how I knew?" He chuckled, almost in embarrassment. "Because she was the only woman who gave me a condition. Can you believe that? She said if you want my company so badly, then *you* should be the person to convince me."

Cole didn't usually care for love stories, but Jonas's had certainly piqued his interest especially since he and Crys had conditions of their own. "So, what did you do?"

Jonas beamed with joy. "I accepted the challenge and convinced her. The rest is history."

Cole frowned. "And that was all it took?"

"Pretty much. The way I see it is if a woman's strong-willed enough to lay down an ultimatum before the relationship has a chance to go anywhere, then she knows what she wants in life. And that, my friend, is a woman worth holding on to. Look, I've learned a lot through the years, and went through my fair share of heartache. When my parents died, I was at a stage where I thought I was invincible. Boy, was I wrong. But I came away realizing that with every door God closes, another opens. The trick is being man enough to walk through it."

Chapter Twenty-two

The next morning, Cole pinched the bridge of his nose as Rhonda continued to bark out orders. Everything had to go off without a hitch, or she was going to skin every man alive who failed Jonas. She made it her personal mission to see this surprise wedding to the end, and with her clipboard in hand, nothing on that spreadsheet had a chance of slipping through the cracks.

Cole couldn't blame her. She was the perfect person for keeping everyone on task. He just wished she could do so without the drill sergeant routine.

As Cole, Rod, and Brody waited for their next assignment, Rhonda took a step back, and swept her gaze over the beautifully decorated dinner tables with systematic scrutiny. "All right, boys, you did well." She checked her watch. "And with three hours to spare. Not bad."

Cole breathed an inward sigh of relief. "Now what do we do?"

Rhonda consulted her clipboard. "Rod and Brody, you

have an hour to get ready. I expect you both to be back here at fourteen hundred hours so you can direct our guests to park in the field behind the barn."

"Yes, ma'am." Rod saluted.

"Brody, don't forget to bring Olivia with you. She'll be stationed to the right of the arbor, and she'll need to get with Jethro for a clip-on mic before she sings. You and your brother will be walking with me down the aisle. Cole, you'll be with Crys. The florist should be here soon," Rhonda said, glancing down the drive. "And there he is. Cole, I'll need you to show him where he can store the flowers until Ava gets here."

As soon as he stepped away with his orders, Rhonda caught him by the arm.

"Is Ava's dress still hanging in your bedroom where I put it?"

Cole rolled his eyes. That damn thing had stared at him all night as he tried to fall asleep, but he didn't dare move it lest he face the wrath of the female tyrant. "I haven't touched it."

"Good. After you assist the florist, you need to head over to Jonas's. He wants to escort his bride to the altar on horseback once she gets here. You and him will be riding Winchester and Ranger from his place to yours after you're both showered and dressed. Keep Jonas on a strict time schedule as I know he's prone to drifting. Oh, and don't forget, you also need to get with Jethro after the ceremony for your clip-on mic. Crys too."

"Why do we need mics?"

Rhonda exhaled in exasperation. "For your toast, Cole. Please tell me you and Crys have a speech lined up."

Cole patted her shoulder gently. "You need to breathe, Rhonda. We've got this."

"Do you? Then what about your dog? He can't roam free with all these people here. You know how he doesn't take well to strangers."

"It's already taken care of. Sammy's going with me to Jonas's, and I'll tie him up there."

"Well then, get a wiggle on!" she replied, slapping her hand against her clipboard. Without hesitation, the three men scattered like worker ants.

****

"Oh, this spa day was wonderful!" Ava exclaimed from inside Crys's truck. She reclined her seat and relished the warmth of the late afternoon sun beaming through her window. "I'm so glad you set this up. What a great idea."

"Rhonda was the one who suggested it," Crys confessed, "so I can't take all the credit."

Ava laughed. "This definitely has Rhonda written all over it. She should've come with us."

Crys gripped her steering wheel a little tighter, hoping she could keep up the ruse. She'd done a bang-up job insofar as Ava still had no idea she'd gotten all dolled-up for her wedding day. "I asked her to, but I think she said something about spending time with her kids this weekend."

"Oh well, her loss."

Ava let out another long sigh, one of the many Crys had heard all day. She took her eyes off the road and checked her friend's appearance. Large bouncy auburn curls, gathered loosely on top of her head, added sophistication and class to her usual ponytail. A French manicure polished the nails often stained and chipped. And seductive smoky-eyes magnified Ava's natural beauty, making her the prettiest rancher in all of Wyoming.

"My God, you look amazing."

Ava sat up and giggled. "I do, don't I? And I'm thrilled that I already know how I'm going to do my makeup and hair for my wedding next year. Talk about taking that stress away."

Crys could hardly contain her smile. "You really like it, huh?"

"Oh, yes. As perfect as this looks, I could get married

today." Ava pulled her visor down and reviewed her reflection in the mirror. "It's a shame I have to wait until next fall. Which reminds me, now that I've picked out the dress I want, we should go ahead and order it. Don't you think?"

Crys stared at the road ahead, worried that if Ava took one look at her, she'd blow it. "Definitely."

Ava slapped the visor back up and stared out her window. "So, where are we headed now?"

"I thought we'd check out a few of the houses I had my eye on, if that's okay with you."

"After these massages we've had today, you won't hear a word of complaint from me."

"Well then, I hope you don't mind if we drop by Cole's place. I accidently left my realty magazine in his truck that night he drove me around Meeteetse. I have a few places I've circled, but I need their addresses for GPS." Crys swallowed, relieving the dryness in her throat. Telling lies, even the little white ones, were so not her forte.

"Like I said," Ava sighed blissfully. "No fuss from me. I'm at your disposal."

Crys grabbed her cell from the console and handed it to Ava. "Can you text Cole and let him know we're almost there. I don't want to surprise that man any more than I have to."

"Sure." Ava punched in the message and sent it through, after which she looked at Crys apologetically.

Crys felt her gaze from across the cab. "What? Why you looking at me like that?"

"I just can't stop thinking about how you and Cole got off on the wrong foot. If it hadn't been for my prying, I really think you two could've hit it off. I probably pushed too hard. And knowing Cole like I do, I shouldn't have intervened."

"It's no big deal. Truly."

"I know you say that, especially now that you've met somebody else, but I hope you know I was only trying to spark some interest for Cole." Ava drummed her fingers on the door and returned to staring out her window. "If only he could've broken his rule…just this once…"

Just this once, Crys wished she could break her promise to Cole and tell Ava that the spark she attempted to light had blazed into a steamy, hot love affair.

Just this once, she wanted to brag about the toe-curling passionate kisses they sneaked when no one was looking.

Just this once, she was dying to pull over and tell it all in explicit detail. But a man like Cole only came around once in a blue moon. To confide in Ava meant destroying everything they'd worked so hard to build, now that she'd gotten him to lower his defensive walls, brick by brick.

****

Cole pulled out his cell upon feeling it vibrate. The moment they'd all been waiting for was about to happen. "It's Crys," he said to Jonas, standing amid a crowd of guests. "They're almost here."

Rhonda lit up with excitement. "Places everyone! Places!"

Jonas shook hands with his brother, Trace, who was dressed in his marine uniform. An unspoken wish of luck and pride shown in his sibling's eyes as Jonas and Cole mounted up. Muted chatter surrounded them as they cued Ranger and Winchester into a trot down the long driveway of Cole's farm.

Cole felt jitters in his stomach, and he had no idea why. It wasn't like he was about to get hitched. He yanked at his collar, loosening the tie that was darn near choking him. He could only imagine how Jonas was feeling in that saddle.

"Any last words, McKinley?"

Jonas laughed heartily. "It's not like I'm a dead man walking, Forester. It's marriage, not a death sentence."

"Same difference."

"Yeah, well, when you find the right woman, you don't

look at it like that."

When they came to a halt at the entrance, Cole heard Jonas give a long exhalation under the creak of leather shifting in his saddle. "For someone who's ready to get married, you sure sound awful nervous over there."

"I'm only nervous that Ava might not take too kindly that I planned her entire wedding without her. What if she's disappointed? What if she says no?"

Cole felt a grin tug on his lips. "Ava won't turn you down. You two are made for each other."

Another long sigh escaped the groom. "That we are."

As Crys's shiny black Denali turned the bend, Cole's heart kicked up. He and Jonas sat frozen in their saddles, watching her pull in and park.

Cole hardly recognized either of the women through the windshield. They both looked like they'd just stepped off the runway of a high-dollar modeling gig. Crys was always a beautiful woman, even without a stick of makeup on. But seeing her in this unusually glamorous state, he nearly fell off his horse as he dismounted.

"My God, she's beautiful," Jonas murmured as he stood beside his horse.

Cole agreed, but he wasn't looking at Ava.

As she and Crys got out of the vehicle, he stared as if he hadn't the ability to do anything else. And he wasn't sorry for it. The gleam in Crys's eyes told him she was just as pleased by his gawking.

"Jonas," Ava said hesitantly as she took in the sight of his formal attire. "What's going on? What are you two all dressed up for?"

Jonas gave his reins to Cole and took Ava by the hand. "Hey, Trick," he said as he so commonly referred to her. "When I proposed to you a few months ago, I was lying beside you on a blanket beneath our tree. Do you remember?"

"How could I forget? It was one of the happiest days of my life."

"Today, I'd like to make you happy again. But this time, I'm going to do it right."

Ava inched closer, glancing between him and Cole. "I don't understand."

Jonas dropped to bended knee as he held her left hand. "Ava, will you marry me?" He paused, then added, "Today?"

Ava's eyes bulged out of her head. "Today? Like...right now?"

"Yes. Right now."

"But I can't get married in jeans, Jonas."

He laughed at her fretting. "You don't have to. I ordered the dress you picked out, and your bridesmaid dresses too. Rhonda took care of altering it, and all you have to do is slip it on."

Ava's hands trembled as tears welled up in her eyes. "But what about your brother? And my mother? They'd want to be here for this."

Crys stepped in and wrapped her arm around Ava's waist. "Everyone is here. Up at Cole's barn."

A light went off in Ava's head. "So that's why Sawyer had me pick him up at the airport. I can't believe this." She cupped Jonas's face. "You did all this for me? To surprise me?"

"I did it all to show you how much I love you."

The second her tears streamed from her eyes, Crys chimed in. "No, no, don't cry. You'll mess up your makeup. Here." She handed Ava a tissue to blot her cheeks and hugged her tight. "Now get on your damn horse and get married."

Ava pulled Jonas to his feet and wept in his arms. "I can't believe I'm getting married today." She walked with him toward Ranger and allowed him to hoist her into her saddle, letting out a joyous whoop. "I'm getting married today!"

Chapter Twenty-three

Rhonda assisted Crys and Ava with their wedding attire and made some last-minute adjustments to their hair and makeup. Standing side by side in front of Cole's bedroom mirror, the three of them took time to breathe, reflect, and smile at how lovely they looked.

Beneath Ava's red flannel shirt tied at the front was a simple white gown with a flattering square neckline, an empire waist, and a cascade of satin-hemmed tulle ruffling the skirt. Under Crys's and Rhonda's short-waisted denim jackets, their dresses were made of sheer rosette lace with a high-low hemline matching Ava's. Each of them planted their hands on their hips and admired the cowboy boots adorning their feet, an extra accessory that topped off the casual-elegant western look Ava had always wanted.

"We look about as cute as can be," Rhonda said as she hip-bumped Ava. "And everything fits perfectly."

Ava smoothed her hands down her hips and regarded her tan, bare leg sticking out from beneath her dress. "You did a fabulous job on the alterations. You think Jonas will like this dress?"

"Oh, child, don't start that again. You know the man finds you absolutely irresistible no matter what you wear. But just in case you still doubt yourself, I recommend staying clear of horse troughs."

The three of them cackled like hens. It would be a long time before anyone forgot about the time Ava had accidentally fallen into a tub of water while trying to seduce Jonas with a wet handkerchief.

"I just wish I could've been there to see it," Crys said, holding her stomach.

As their laughter slowly subsided, Sawyer burst through the front door. "Hey, Mom!" he called up to the loft. "Are you gals about ready? Jonas is getting pretty antsy out here. He said, and I quote, tell Trick to get her damn ass out here."

"That sounds like my Jonas," Ava answered back. "I'm coming." She took one more glance in the mirror and hugged her friends. "Thank you both for everything you've done to help Jonas pull this off. It may have been his idea, but I know he couldn't have done it without your help. Thank you so much."

"All right, all right," Rhonda rushed. "You've got guests waiting and a groom chomping at the bit."

"Oh, Mom," Sawyer drawled out as he came to the top of the stairs. "You look amazing."

Ava melted at her son's compliment, and she kissed his cheek. "Thank you, sweetheart."

Sawyer swiveled on his heel and stuck out his elbow. "Shall I give you away?"

Ava smiled and linked her arm in his. Together they walked down the stairs and out the front door. Brody and Rod both tipped their hats to the bride before stepping inside for Rhonda.

"My, my," Rhonda said, fanning her face. "Don't you boys clean up mighty nice."

Rod took a gander at Crys and Rhonda as they descended the stairs and blew out a long whistle. "You ladies don't look half-bad yourselves. I hope one of you beauties will save me a dance."

"You can bet your sweet ass I will," Rhonda said, grabbing Rod's butt.

Crys giggled when she caught a glimpse of Rod's exaggerated look of fright before he and Brody escorted her out the door. To add to her delight, Cole stepped in, looking twice as fearful.

"Now, that's a woman who's about to cut loose."

"Lord help all the single men out there," Crys joked.

Cole removed his newly pressed Stetson and blew out

his own whistle. "I hope he helps me first, 'cause I'm going need all the divine intervention I can get to keep my hands off you."

Crys linked her arm into Cole's extended elbow, wondering how she was going to do the same. With his crisp white shirt, light blue tie, and tight black jeans, it was going to take a more than a miracle to resist her sharply dressed cowboy.

****

Cole had a heck of time walking Crys down the aisle. She smelled like a strawberry patch, ripe for the picking on a dewy summer morning. Added in her dramatic, smoky makeup, and it was easy for him to fantasize about her in ways he shouldn't, especially when there was a sea of faces staring at him.

He scanned the crowd. Everyone was dressed to the hilt and genuinely joyous for this special ceremony uniting Jonas and Ava in marriage.

As he and Crys separated and stood on opposite sides of the arbor, he pondered his obsession with Crys. Perhaps he felt he had to have her every waking moment simply because he couldn't. Their relationship was a secret. And his heart broke little by little each time they parted ways.

Making matters worse, he missed her like crazy when she was gone.

As foreign as all those emotions felt to him, he seemed more unsettled by her plans to buy a place of her own. He hated to think that they'd still have separate lives and separate beds to go home to. Nothing would change between them.

Normally, he preferred monotony. When things stayed the same, there was less risk of complications or surprises. But who knew he'd be ready to be someone's boyfriend? Who knew he'd want to wake up to the same woman's face every morning? Who knew how strong he felt about Crys in his life?

Yes, she was the only woman he'd ever truly cared for, but did that mean she was *the one*?

He brought to mind the conversation he and Jonas had yesterday about knowing when the right person comes along. He never knew the difference because, until Crys, every woman was virtually the same. They either tried to change him or didn't care enough to make an effort beyond the feat of sleeping with him.

Crys, however, was a godsend in that she didn't direct his lifestyle to coincide with hers. And because she allowed him that freedom, he found himself thinking about their longevity and where his future was headed should they stay together.

He watched Jonas and Ava dismount from their horses and enter the barn, arm in arm, beneath the twinkling lights that he and Crys had strung, and he wondered if Crys had been the right woman for him all along and he was too self-absorbed to see it.

Images of her working long hours in his barn without complaint bounced around in his head. He couldn't believe the painstaking hours she'd spent helping him get this barn in tip-top shape, or, even still, that he'd ever be caught dead hot-gluing daisies and burlap strips on mason jars for table decorations.

But he gladly did it all with Crys.

She filled a void in his life he never knew existed. As much as he'd love to deny it, Crys made him whole. And every rule be damned, he had to find a way to tell her how he felt, once and for all.

****

Crys's heart swelled as Ava and Jonas stood before their friends and family, ready to publicly profess their love and devotion to each other. It amazed her to think how much trouble Jonas had gone through to create the perfect wedding day for his beloved. He was a man who wasn't afraid of commitment or sacrifice, and he understood the value of having someone special to share life's journey with.

As she cast her gaze in Cole's direction, she wished he was more like Jonas. She'd give anything to hear him publicly admit he couldn't live without her. That every night they kissed good-bye was like a knife in his heart.

She was tired of feeling that knife in her own heart, and the only way to make it stop was to tell Cole how she felt.

As she closed her eyes, his words, oh so precious to her ears, echoed in her head: *I can't remember my life before you. All I know is you. All I need is you.*

"Dearly beloved," the local pastor greeted with outstretched arms.

At the priest's loud, booming voice, Crys opened her eyes and tried to keep her focus on the bride and groom.

"We are gathered here today to witness the union of Jonas Murphy McKinley and Ava Evangeline Wallace in the bonds of holy matrimony, which is an honorable estate that is not to be entered into unadvisedly or lightly, but reverently and soberly.

"Into this estate, these two persons present come now to be joined. If anyone can show just cause why they may not be lawfully joined together, let them speak now or forever hold their peace."

Though Crys did not intend to speak out against this marriage, she decided she could no longer hold her peace about her feelings for Cole. All she needed was a moment alone with him.

Chapter Twenty-four

When Jonas and Ava shared their first kiss as husband and wife, Crys felt jittery inside. And when she sat beside the couple at the dinner table with a full plate of food, she could barely eat. Though she knew weddings were a time to mingle with family and friends and be cordial with those she'd just met, all she could think about was talking with Cole.

After two hours of tedious socializing, Jonas and his brother caught up with her.

"This is Major Trace McKinley," he introduced.

"Please," his brother said, shaking her hand. "Call me Trace."

He stood tall and dignified in his dress blues, with his white cap tucked beneath his arm. Countless pins and insignias adorned his jacket, and Crys couldn't begin to know what any of them were for.

She tried to feign interest in finally getting to meet a man who devoted his life to the service of his country. She asked him the usual questions, like where he was currently stationed and how long he'd be there. But regardless of how special it was that Trace had flown in for his brother's wedding, or that he was extremely handsome—and single—her attention was continually drawn to Cole as he circulated from person to person.

She'd just about given up, when she saw him stroll across the yard. She darted to catch him but wasn't fast enough. As soon as he joined Rod, Brody, and Olivia, she turned on her heel and struck up a conversation with Ava's mother, who stood nearby.

As Mrs. Wallace droned on about the good old days when Crys and Ava toured the rodeo circuit, she spotted Cole heading toward the DJ table. He and Jethro talked for a few minutes, then Jethro fiddled with Cole's tie.

"Excuse me, Mrs. Wallace," Rhonda interrupted. "May I steal Crys from you a second? She needs to give her toast with the best man."

"Certainly, dear." Ava's mother patted Crys's back. "We'll talk later, hon. Good luck up there."

Rhonda pulled Crys aside. "Did you get your clip-on mic from Jethro?"

Crys stammered. "Uh, no. I didn't know I needed one."

Rhonda groaned. "I told Cole this morning that he

needed to make sure you got with Jethro about it. Look, Cole's up there right now getting his. Hurry, so Ava and Jonas can cut the cake."

****

Cole patted his pockets, looking for the toast he'd written on a piece of paper. *Shit.* He must have left it in the house.

With his hand over the mic, he leaned toward Jethro. "Can I walk away from this table? I forgot my cheat sheet."

"You're fine," Jethro insisted as he pushed buttons and turned dials on his soundboard. "It's wireless. Just don't say anything between now and then. In about two minutes, I should have you up and running."

Cole made a mad dash for his house, hoping he could find it. He'd never be able to deliver his heartfelt toast on the fly without it.

As he burst through his door and jetted up the stairs, he could feel the prickle of perspiration in his pores. Clothes, makeup—and yes, even a few tampons in their packaging; most likely a gag from Rhonda—were strewn about his bed and floor. He ignored it all and scavenged his bedroom.

Ripping drawers open in a panic, he finally found it in

his nightstand. He turned to rush back and collided with Crys, catching her before she hit the floor.

"I'm so sorry, Crys. Are you all right?"

"Yes, yes, I'm fine." Crys caught her breath and smiled. "I just needed to talk to you. Finally, we're alone."

Cole freaked, remembering that Jethro had wired him with a mic. "Crys, wait—"

"No, I'm talking first. I've waited all evening to have you to myself, and I'm not—"

"Crys, please," he begged. "You don't understand."

"I *do* understand. But your rule is hardly a rule anymore, especially since you broke it to be with me. And I've tried to be patient, but I can't take it anymore. You need to know exactly how I feel."

He grabbed her by the arms and pinned her with a hardened glare. "Seriously. Not now."

"If not now, when? When, Cole?" Crys jerked out of his hold and paced the bedroom. "You've had every opportunity to tell your friends that we've been seeing each other for the past seven weeks, and you haven't taken it."

"Don't say another word." He tried to remove the mic from his tie, but it snagged. He made a desperate attempt to remove the tie from his neck, but the knot was too tight, and he was all thumbs.

"Look, I get that this is hard for you, but I can't go on,

feeling the way I do."

Crys stopped pacing, and now that she stared at him, he gave up on the tie. "Don't do this," he pleaded.

She ignored him. "I've fallen for you, Cole. I've fallen hard, and I really think you feel the same."

Cole's heart hammered in his chest. He didn't know what to do or what to say now that the cat was out of the bag. All he could do was pray his mic wasn't on.

"I don't expect you to admit it, especially since I've just blindsided you." She slowly moved toward him and gathered his hands in hers. "But try to realize that what we have doesn't come by easily or often. We're great together. And every person out there," she pointed, "especially Jonas and Ava, would agree if they only knew. You said yourself, you're perfectly happy when you're with me. So, let's quit this stupid charade and tell them."

Cole hung his head. "It's possible you already have."

From the brim of his hat, he watched Crys's brow squish together in confusion. "No, I haven't. I've told no one. Not even Ava."

"Trust me when I tell you, everyone probably knows."

"How is that possible?"

Cole tapped the little black clip on his tie. "My mic is on. Well, it's supposed to be."

Crys stared at him, speechless. She touched her hand

to the base of her neck and peered over his loft in the direction of his front door below. Though he couldn't tell what she was thinking, he could hear her wheels turning. Hoping he was wrong about the mic, he followed her down the stairs and stood behind her as she opened the door.

A crowd of people, looking about as expectant as a group of lotto participants waiting for the perfect number combination to be called, stared at them. Slow smiles split their lips in unison, but no one said a word.

Ava rushed to the front and scaled Cole's porch steps. She reached for Crys's hand, and glanced between them. "Is this true?"

Crys covered her face and groaned. "I can't believe this."

"Neither can I," Cole said, squeezing through the door. "I need a beer."

"Cole, wait!"

He stopped abruptly and yanked on the clip, ripping his tie. He handed the mic to Ava and deferred giving his toast. "I'm sorry." As he looked out over the disappointed crowd, he stepped off his porch and escaped the awkward whispers that surrounded him.

Chapter Twenty-five

Crys sat on Cole's porch bench with her head in her hands. Ava and Rhonda rubbed her back and offered their best condolences. Wedding or not, it felt more like a funeral as she died a thousand times over in humiliation.

What killed her the most was knowing she might have destroyed her one chance to be with Cole the way she wanted. Why couldn't she just have been patient and waited until after the wedding to talk with him? Why couldn't she have kept her damn mouth shut?

"Crys, honey," Ava soothed. "You can't beat yourself up for this. This is Cole's issue, not yours. If he can't admit his feelings for you, then you shouldn't waste anymore of your life with him. You're a wonderful woman and probably the best thing that's ever happened to him, but if he can't see that, then you don't need him."

"I never needed him, Ava. I just fell in love with him, and he's too scared to face it." Crys raised her head and glanced over the wedding guests, who'd gone back to celebrating what was left of Ava and Jonas's special day. The sight of Cole and Jonas deep in conversation along the distant fence line ate at her insides. "I should've known better. For crying out loud, it wasn't as if he didn't warn me."

Ava squeezed her shoulder. "I'm sorry that it came out this way."

Crys hugged her friend as she coped with guilt. "I'm so sorry I ruined your wedding."

"You didn't ruin anything."

"Maybe not, but I still want to crawl into a hole."

"Sounds like you could use a drink," Rhonda said, standing. "I'll get you one."

"Make it stiff."

As Rhonda headed into the crowd of people, Crys saw Cole drawing near. Ava looked up and saw the same. There was a look of sheer determination on Cole's face as he downed his beer and skirted the guests.

"I'll handle this," Ava said.

Crys stood and caught her friend's wrist in protest.

"Just relax," Ava reassured.

Easier said than done. Crys's heart was so far up in her throat, she thought she'd puke. When Cole made it to the porch, he slid his gaze from Crys to Ava, giving her a look that meant *step aside.*

"Cole, I don't think this is the time or the place. Perhaps, tomorrow you can—"

"Tomorrow's too late. I'd like to talk to Crys, now."

When Cole didn't budge, Ava looked to her husband for backup. "Jonas?"

He stepped forward and wrapped his arm around his wife's shoulder. "Just let the man speak. Okay?"

Crys glared at Jonas. Without Ava as her shield, she felt vulnerable in front of Cole. Adding the weight of stares from those behind him, she sprang like a cornered rat. "Save it. I know what you're going to say."

Cole smiled smugly. "No you don't."

He crossed his arms, and she rolled her eyes. "Fine. Get it over with."

"I intend to. And I hope you're listening, Crys, 'cause I'm only going to say this once."

She braced herself for the good-bye.

"Ever since I met you, you've turned my world upside down, and that was exactly what I was trying to avoid. You know I hate complications and drama. And you know I like things the way they are. Yet, somehow, I let you convince me to break my rule. The one rule that would've kept all this," he gestured with a wide open sweep of his arms, "from happening."

Crys lowered her head. She couldn't look at him

anymore. It hurt too much to hear these words from a man she thought cared for her.

"And I thank God you did," he added.

Crys lifted her gaze and noticed a tiny smile inching on his lips. And not the smug kind like before, but a genuine, sweet sort of grin she wasn't used to seeing. Though her heart beat wildly, she was still a little gun-shy over the way he'd initiated this whole lecture. "What are you saying?"

"I'm saying...I love you."

Before she could process his words, he lunged forward and captured her lips in a kiss hot enough to set his porch on fire. Tears of joy streamed from her eyes, but Cole brushed them away, erasing all doubt and sadness from her once troubled heart.

Their kiss was long and passionate. Cheers and applause rang out around them, and still, he never broke the kiss. It wasn't until Olivia's voice came over the speakers that he pulled away.

"I'd like to make a toast," she bellowed out. "It is said that love does not consist of gazing at each other, but in looking outward together in the same direction. So here's to Jonas and Ava, and Cole and Crys. May you always look to the future, and may you always find love and happiness."

****

Crys couldn't stop gazing into Cole's eyes as they danced to the sweet musical talents of Olivia Langston, soon-to-be country music sensation. As everyone swayed and whispered in their partners' ears, Crys was content to admire the cowboy who made her the happiest woman in the state of Wyoming.

"Can I ask you something?" Crys asked dreamily.

"Do I have to answer?"

Crys laughed at his joke. "Yes, you do. And no lies, no games."

It was Cole's turn to laugh. "Touché."

She stroked the sharp angles of his scruffy face, relishing the fact that she could finally touch him in plain sight. "Why did you walk away and leave me to think the worst? If you loved me, why didn't you just tell me?"

Cole looked up to the sky and sighed. "You have to understand, I hate to be the center of attention. And when I saw all those people staring at me, I froze up. I couldn't speak if I wanted to. Not to mention, you stole my thunder. I had already planned on telling you how I felt, but I just needed a little time to figure out how. I didn't have the words. I hope you can forgive me."

"I do."

"Good. Now it's my turn to ask you something." He

spun her around and dipped her over his arm. He waited for her laughter to subside, then planted a kiss on her lips. "Will you stay with me?"

Crys narrowed her gaze, wondering why he felt the need to ask when it was no longer necessary to sleep at different residences. "I kind of planned on it, cowboy."

"No, I mean stay with me, as in live here," he clarified.

Bent over his arm, Crys grabbed hold of his shirt and pulled herself to a standing position. "You want me to *live* with you?"

Cole nodded his head matter-of-factly. "I do, and what's mine is yours."

Crys couldn't believe what she was hearing. "But why?"

He twirled her body once and drew her back in his embrace. "Because I love you. Plain and simple." He nipped her nose and smiled. "If you still want to buy your own place, I won't stop you. And I'll support your decision if that's what you think is best."

She looked at him askance. "Am I dreaming?"

"If you're not sure about this, just at least move your truck and trailer to my place until you figure it all out. Can you do that?"

Crys wrapped her arms around his neck. "I reckon I can. On one condition."

Cole threw his head back and laughed. "This again?"

"You scared?"

He adjusted his cowboy hat, then said, "No, ma'am, I'm not. Whatcha got in mind, Angel?"

"I'll move in with you…"

"If?" he baited.

"If you take me out shooting. With a rifle."

Cole furrowed his brow. "That's it?"

"Yep."

He still looked skeptical. "What are we shooting?"

"Your choice. Targets can be as big or as little as you want. And maybe, just maybe…if I'm good enough with a rifle, we can shoot targets for favors."

"Now, that shines!"

Chapter Twenty-six

One week later

Crys watched Cole trot across the valley on Jail. As usual, Sammy sat at her feet, waiting for his owner to return from setting up a twenty-four-inch-diameter bull's-eye target about fifty yards away, and four cans of beer along the top. There was something about a cowboy on his horse that turned her insides to mush, especially one dressed in chaps and a slicker. He reminded her of the old Clint Eastwood movies she used to watch with her brothers when she was younger.

"You sure you're ready for fifty yards?" he asked as he dismounted. "It's okay if you want to start out at thirty, since this is your first time."

She brought her hand up to her brow to shade the glare of the sun as she peered across the meadow. "No, I think it's fine for now. If I can't hit it, we can always move it in."

Cole strolled over to her and took the rifle from her hands. "I'll shoot first, and then I'll show you."

"Okay, Clint. Whatever you say."

She watched him raise the barrel and position the stock in his shoulder pocket, while he spread his feet to a comfortable stance. He began instructing her about proper cheek weld, something she'd never do with a shotgun because of its recoil, but she zoned out. Though the slicker he wore draped below the back of his knees, she couldn't help but ogle him.

"Crys?"

She looked up and realized Cole had caught her staring.

"Focus on the target. Not my butt."

"Sorry."

He sighed and went back to instructing her on the basics of trigger control, accuracy, and consistency. She listened to him and never made a peep, giving him the respect and attention he deserved for being a skilled marksman.

After he popped off five shots, he lowered his weapon and handed it to her. "Remember, breathe in, breathe out, then press the trigger. Don't pull. It'll alter your sights."

"Right." She shook out her feet and stretched her neck. "Now don't laugh if I miss."

Cole stood behind her. "Where's your confidence?"

"I have confidence," Crys contended. "I'm just a little nervous."

"Angel, I've seen you with a shotgun. It's evident you know the fundamentals of shooting. So, quit hangin' fire and show me what you got."

Crys felt his proximity when she got into her stance and looked into the scope. She breathed in and out, just as Cole had coached her to do, but dropped her sights. "I can't do this with you looking over my shoulder."

Immediately, Cole backed up. "Sorry."

When he stood a few feet behind her, she turned and tried again. She closed her left eye, and peered with her dominant right, taking notice of Cole's impressive bullet pattern. Every one hit dead center.

She lowered the rifle again and glanced over her shoulder at him.

"What now?" he asked.

"We forgot to lay wagers."

Cole snickered. "Don't you think it's best to wait until you've shot at least once? I'd hate for you to lose straight out of the gate."

"What, are you scared?"

"No, I'm just saying that I think we should save the high stakes bets for when you're ready."

Crys moved out of a shooting stance and into a safe resting position with the butt of the rifle planted firmly on the ground. Holding fast to the barrel, she called Cole out. "Are you so proud that you think I can't win?"

"No…"

"Then tell me your fantasy." She waited, and when he didn't give it up, she coaxed him harder. "Come on, come on. I want to know what excites you."

He hesitated, then said, "Well, you know how you had that dark makeup around your eyes…that sexy, sultry look the night of Jonas and Ava's wedding?"

"The smoky eye?"

"Yeah," he said hungrily. "I'd really like to see that again. But with you looking up at me like you did in that stall."

Crys smiled, happy that he'd confided in her. "I can do that. In fact, I'll do that every night for a month—if I lose, of course."

She watched him swallow as he shifted his weight to the other leg.

"E-every night? For a whole month? Crys, that's a little extreme, don't you think?"

"But if I win…" she contested. "You have to cook me breakfast every morning for a month. Naked."

Cole laughed uneasily. "You're talking seriously high

stakes here, Crys. You sure you don't want to rip out a few shots first?"

She slumped her shoulders. "Yeah, you're probably right." After a little contemplation, she lifted the gun by the forestock and repositioned her stance. She looked into her scope and fired her first shot.

She closed her eyes and lowered the barrel. "I don't want to look. Tell me how I did."

Cole took out his binoculars and peered at the bull's-eye. "Um, I don't think you even hit it."

"Crap. I think I pulled the trigger. Can I have a do-over?"

"Sure. It's a common rookie mistake." He adjusted his hat and looked at her sympathetically. "We can even forget about the wager this time if you want."

"No, no, the bet still stands. But how about the best two out of three?"

"Crys, this doesn't feel right. What kind of man would I be gambling against a beginner?"

"Can I have two more shots or not?"

Cole groaned. "Take your shot. Hell, take ten. But just know, you're the one who set the bar too high."

"Fine," she said, lifting the rifle. "I'll take your ten…" One right after another, she laid waste to his pattern in the center of the bull's-eye until six shots rang out. She then raised the muzzle a few inches and took aim at the row of beer cans on top. One by one, the four cans danced off the ledge with beer foam squirting everywhere. "…and I'll raise you breakfast." She handed Cole the rifle and smiled. "I like my eggs scrambled, please."

Cole raised his binoculars again and checked the bull's-eye in doubt. When he saw that she'd annihilated his five shots as well as the row of cans, he shook his head as she walked away.

"Did you just hustle me?"

Crys laughed as she sauntered. "Did you forget to bring your A game, cowboy?"

Chapter Twenty-seven

Brody killed the engine of his truck and gazed out over the Grand Tetons jetting high above the Jackson Hole Airport. He'd come to dread this location as it became the place for saying farewell to Liv for an undetermined amount of time, and he wasn't quite ready to let her go.

The precious moments they'd spent together, though it had been a couple of months, went by so fast. Yet whenever she was away in Nashville, those days crept along like molasses in winter.

As he sat in silence, he wondered how many times he'd have to go through this before he'd get used to it. He liked to think this time might be different as he refused to sit in his truck and watch her plane glide down the runway any longer.

He felt the seat give as she inched closer. When he looked at her, he saw he wasn't the only one having a hard time. A tear fell from her eye and trickled down her pretty face. He reached across and wiped it tenderly away.

"I don't want you to cry, Liv."

"I don't want to say good-bye," she said, holding fast to his hand. "I wish I could take you with me."

A grin tugged on his lips. He'd been waiting so long for this moment, and he couldn't believe how easily, and unknowingly, she baited him. "Then why don't you?"

Liv sighed long and hard. "I'd give anything if that were possible. I even contemplated asking you, but I know the answer."

"Do you?"

"Of course, I do. We've been through this before." Liv leaned back against the seat and closed her eyes. "Your life is here. Your job is on the McKinley ranch. I could never expect you to uproot from Meeteetse for me."

"What if," he began as he toyed with a strand of her long, dark hair, "I visited you every now and again?"

"I would love that."

Brody watched her shrug her shoulders, a reaction to a question she obviously thought was purely hypothetical. He smiled at her. "What if now and again was today?"

Her eyes flashed open, and she pinned him with a scowl. "Don't kid me like that, Galven."

"I'm not kidding."

Liv bolted upright and yanked him so hard by the collar of his shirt that she wrenched him forward. "What are you saying? Are you actually thinking of coming to Nashville with me? Right now?"

He couldn't help but laugh at her. "There's no thinking about it. It's a done deal. I bought my plane ticket last week and my suitcase is packed in the bed of my truck, that is if you don't mind me tagging along."

Liv leapt into his lap and bear-hugged him, causing his horn to blare and his cowboy hat to tumble to the floorboard. Brody waved an apology to the passerby in the parking lot, but continued to embrace the exuberant woman squealing in his arms. He tried to shush her, but it was no use.

"Galven, you are the best! I can't believe you're coming to Nashville with me, I could just scream!"

Brody covered his ear and cringed. "I believe you did."

"I'm sorry, I'm just so happy. And surprised! What made you decide to do this?"

"Actually, it was your mother's idea."

Liv froze. "It was?"

Brody was just as shocked when June had mentioned it one night after he'd dropped Liv off at her mama's house. They'd talked over a cup of coffee on the front porch about his plans, Liv's future, and how he intended to make a long distance relationship work. "I think your mama was testing me to see if I was in this for the long haul, but I thought, why not? I could use a vacation."

"But what about your job?"

"Winter's coming, which means things will start to slow down after the first heavy snowfall. Jonas said if I'm going to take some time off, now's my chance."

Looking him straight in the eye, Liv addressed him with a serious tone in her voice. "Are you sure this is what you want to do?"

"I know I don't want to watch you fly away again from the parking lot of this damn airport. And if that means I have to get on that plane with you, then I reckon I'm Nashville bound. 'Course I might draw some attention," he added, glancing at his colorfully inked sleeves.

Liv stroked his forearms. "Trust me, you're not the only tattooed cowboy in Tennessee. You'll fit right in, don't worry."

He blew out a heavy breath. "The only thing I'm worried about is being trapped at thirty thousand feet with no escape."

She pulled back. "Brody Galven, are you afraid of flying?"

He hated to admit it, but yes. He was petrified. He'd rather break a vicious wild horse sure to fracture every bone in his body than sit pretty in a first class plane seat. "I might be a little nervous."

Liv made a sound of pity and kissed his lips. "You'll be fine. I'll even hold your hand the whole time if you'd like."

Brody brought to mind the conversation he had with his brother when he told him he was heading to Nashville. "Rod said if I'm still nervous after take-off, that you should introduce me to the mile-high club. What is that?"

Liv broke out into joyous laughter. "That sounds like Rod."

He watched as she climbed out of his lap and reached for her purse with no further explanation. "No seriously, Liv, what is it?"

She opened the door to his truck and climbed out. "I'll tell you all about it after takeoff. Right now, let's just get you through security."

Brody snagged his hat from the floor, dusted it off, and stepped outside. His mind spun as he righted his Stetson on his head and took another long look at the jagged rocky mountain peaks cutting into the blue sky. As he grabbed his suitcase and helped Liv with hers, he couldn't help but think there was more to his brother's suggestion than what it implied.

"Are you a member of the mile-high club?"

Liv wrapped her arm around his waist and giggled as they made their way to the airport lobby doors. "Can't say that I am, Galven, but if there's one thing I've learned about being your girl, it's that there's always a first for everything."

THE END

AUTHOR'S NOTE

Did you know there are two books that come before this one? Sure, my Mavericks of Meeteetse series can be read as stand-alone novels, but the first two introduce some of the hunky cowboys who work the McKinley Ranch.

In *Longing For Langston*, you find out how Meeteetse's bad boy, Brody Galven (one of the hired hands) and his best friend, Liv Langston come together and why they're in the midst of a long-distance relationship.

In *Made For McKinley*, I take you on a journey through the trials and tribulations of Jonas and Ava's seven-year-long relationship, and her hilarious failed attempts at spicing things up.

*All are meant to be stand-alones (and can be read in any order), but for a more satisfying "happily ever after," reading in order is helpful and encouraged.

****

Take a trip out West and meet Brody, Jonas, and Cole—the three sexy, rugged cowboys who rope and run the McKinley ranch, as well as the women who try to tame them.

MAVERICKS OF MEETEETSE
A cowboy romance series set in the small town of
Meeteetse, Wyoming.

Longing For Langston, Novella Book 1
Made for McKinley, Book 2
Falling for Forester, Book 3

LONGING FOR LANGSTON
Mavericks of Meeteetse, Novella Book 1 (Brody & Liv)

Tired of living in his brother's shadow, Brody Galven wants the folks of Meeteetse to realize he's no longer a bad boy screwup. He also wants his childhood best friend, Olivia Langston. While staying out of trouble proves impossible, admitting he loves her is out of the question. But will he still feel that way when she's about to walk out of his life forever?

MADE FOR McKINLEY
Mavericks of Meeteetse, Book 2 (Jonas & Ava)

Former trick rider Ava Wallace works the five-thousand-acre McKinley ranch and loves the man who owns it. Only trouble is, they've been living together for over seven years, and she can't help but think things have changed between them. Her rough-and-tough cowboy used to be relentless with his affection, unable to keep his hands off her. Now, he barely has the time.

Cowboy cattle rancher Jonas McKinley can't seem to catch a break. Between his hardworking live-in girlfriend feeling like they don't connect and the nuisance grizzly that keeps tormenting his livestock, he must overcome the troublesome challenges that threaten his lucrative family farm before he loses what he's worked so hard to keep. Faced with a difficult choice, Jonas has to decide what matters most: Ava or his ranch.

ABOUT THE AUTHOR

RENEE VINCENT is a *USA Today* bestselling author of romance and women's fiction. Her books have earned numerous accolades, including a #1 Bestseller for Viking Romance.

She lives on a secluded hundred-acre horse farm in the rolling hills of Kentucky with her husband, two beautiful daughters, and a few fur babies who've managed to weasel their way into a couple of books.

When she's not writing, she loves to decorate (and redecorate) her home, knit cozy blankets, send homemade cards to family and friends, and concoct her own versions of recipes to pass down to her girls.

www.ReneeVincent.com

Books By Series

Vikings of Honor Series
Sunset Fire, Book 1
Emerald Glory, Book 2
Souls Reborn, Book 3
Tempered Steel, Book 4

Mavericks of Meeteetse Series
Longing for Langston, Brody & Liv, Book 1
Made for McKinley, Jonas & Ava, Book 2
Falling For Forester, Cole & Crys, Book 3

Jamett & Joseph Series
The Start of Something Good, Book 1
The Road to Something Better, Book 2
The Gift of Something Grand, Book 3
Something's Bound to Happen, Books 1 - 3

Stand Alone Novel
Silent Partner

If you enjoyed this book by Renee Vincent, please consider leaving an honest review at your favorite vendor. Reviews not only give credibility to an author's work, they also help other readers find quality books worth reading.

ReneeVincent.com